Y0-BUD-074

SPECIAL MESSAGE TO READERS

This book is published under the auspices of

THE ULVERSCROFT FOUNDATION

(registered charity No. 264873 UK)

Established in 1972 to provide funds for research, diagnosis and treatment of eye diseases. Examples of contributions made are: —

A Children's Assessment Unit at Moorfield's Hospital, London.

•

Twin operating theatres at the Western Ophthalmic Hospital, London.

•

A Chair of Ophthalmology at the Royal Australian College of Ophthalmologists.

•

The Ulverscroft Children's Eye Unit at the Great Ormond Street Hospital For Sick Children, London.

You can help further the work of the Foundation by making a donation or leaving a legacy. Every contribution, no matter how small, is received with gratitude. Please write for details to:

THE ULVERSCROFT FOUNDATION,
The Green, Bradgate Road, Anstey,
Leicester LE7 7FU, England.
Telephone: (0116) 236 4325

In Australia write to:
THE ULVERSCROFT FOUNDATION,
c/o The Royal Australian College of
Ophthalmologists,
27, Commonwealth Street, Sydney,
N.S.W. 2010.

A TIME TO LOVE

After a broken romance, Kate Howard writes off all men as untrustworthy and decides to leave Cape Town to stay with her parents, who live in farming country near the Umvoti River. When Kate is asked to temporarily run the local nursery school, she again meets Peter Watson, the guardian of four-year-old Vicky. He had infuriated Kate from the very first time she had set eyes on him, but she finds it becoming increasingly difficult not to fall in love with this handsome man.

Books by Beverley Winter
in the Linford Romance Library:

HOUSE ON THE HILL

BEVERLEY WINTER

A TIME
TO LOVE

Complete and Unabridged

LINFORD
Leicester

First published in Great Britain

First Linford Edition
published 2003

Copyright © 1998 by Beverley Winter
All rights reserved

British Library CIP Data

Winter, Beverley
   A time to love.—Large print ed.—
Linford romance library
1. Love stories
2. Large type books
I. Title
823.9'14 [F]

ISBN 0–7089–9434–2

Published by
F. A. Thorpe (Publishing)
Anstey, Leicestershire

Set by Words & Graphics Ltd.
Anstey, Leicestershire
Printed and bound in Great Britain by
T. J. International Ltd., Padstow, Cornwall

This book is printed on acid-free paper

1

It was a perfect evening but Kate scarcely noticed. She stumbled over a pile of rotting kelp on the shoreline and stared blankly as the flies rose in buzzing protest only to subside once more when they realised she was no more interested in them than they were in her.

James, of all people! How could he?

A teasing wind flung the salt spray against her cheeks, already damp with tears. Fiercely she dashed them away and glared at the endless white sands of Blouberg Strand stretching into the half-light, pounded by the incessant, icy waters of the Atlantic.

No use moping, was it? They say love is blind. Well, she'd been blind! She wasn't the first woman to have been taken in, of course, but what rankled was that he hadn't actually left her for another woman!

She turned curiously to see again the man who was brooding at the water's edge, shoulders hunched against the wind, dark body blighting the pale foam. He'd been there for ages, too, staring into the ocean, oblivious even of the charming antics of a pair of seals diving in the waves.

The sun sank low and she caught her breath as the light began dying over South Africa's Table Mountain, bathing its sombre slopes where they plunged into the sea. Instinctively she glanced at her left hand where usually the rosy light caressed its cluster of sapphires. Now it only revealed a pale, tell-tale mark which echoed the emptiness in her heart.

She turned bleakly towards the carpark. and shivered as she quickened her pace. When she reached her car, she scrabbled in the pocket of her shorts for the key, dismayed to find that it wasn't there! This was too much! She would just have to retrace her steps. Turning, she gave a yelp of pure fright.

'Yours, I take it? You ought to be more careful.'

The moon had broken through a patch of cloud to reveal the tall figure behind her. It was the stranger from the beach.

'You startled me!' she exclaimed. 'Don't you know better than to creep up on people like that? Yes, that is my key.'

She snatched it from his outstretched hand.

He had spoken with apparent indifference and his voice was deep velvet. He began to feel in his pocket for his own key, his large body merging darkly with the saloon behind him, shoulders still hunched against the wind. He was pinning her once more with that gaze, in no seeming hurry to be gone.

'Why's a woman like you mooching on a deserted beach at night?'

'I beg your pardon? I was simply taking a walk. From my perspective, you were the one who was mooching!'

'That's different. I am a man.'

'So?' Kate flung back at him. 'I always walk here and will continue to do so when I please. Goodnight.'

'It's not exactly safe,' he persisted.

'It's perfectly safe! Anyway, it's none of your business.'

'Perhaps not, but I would be failing in common decency if I neglected to advise you to exercise a little caution in future. You're an attractive woman,' he drawled, 'and all alone.'

Kate scrambled into the driving seat and locked the door with a decided click, disconcerted to notice the flash of amusement in his eyes. Her car jerked forward and with her nose in the air Kate sped away.

Back in her apartment, she couldn't settle. Even her favourite programme proved boring so she switched it off. What on earth was she to do with the rest of the evening? Anything would be preferable to sitting around thinking of James. A curious thought then struck her.

4

For the past half hour it hadn't been James she'd been thinking of, but a stranger on a lonely beach. She jumped as the telephone shrilled. Her greeting was abrupt as she answered.

'Fine way to greet your friends,' Pippa said.

'Sorry, Pip. It's been somewhat of a bad day.'

'Never mind. Auntie Philippa is about to make your dreams come true. I've managed to get tickets for 'Macbeth'. Remember?'

'Oh! Of course. Well, that's nice. When?'

'Tomorrow evening, if you'll call for me. We can have a meal afterwards at that new place on the waterfront I was telling you about.'

'Fine.'

'Kate, are you OK? You don't exactly sound like yourself.'

'I'm fine.'

'Has James upset you again? You haven't ditched him, by any chance?'

'No,' Kate snapped. 'If you must

know, Pippa, it was the other way round. Good-night!'

'Cold as a fish, I always thought,' Pippa remarked the following evening. 'None of us could fathom what you saw in him, Kate. Hang on.'

She paused on the theatre steps and delved into her evening bag.

'I promised my cousin I'd give this package to her boyfriend who is working backstage, one of the technicians. Wait for me in the foyer.'

As she disappeared through a side door, Kate went into the building. It wasn't every day one had the opportunity of seeing Felicia Watson as Lady Macbeth. Even the photographic display in the foyer couldn't do justice to the woman's beauty.

'You'll never guess what I've just seen!' Pippa breathed in her ear. 'The most gorgeous specimen, coming out of Felicia's dressing-room, and in the most foul mood! Tall, dark, in black leather, he was, with a face to match. My cousin's boyfriend says the men are simply falling over themselves for Felicia Watson's favours. This one looked as though he'd fallen flat on his face. And there she was at the door with next to nothing on, yelling at him!'

'Well, whatever her performance offstage,' Kate commented dryly, 'we're bound to get a good one on. Shall we go in?'

A few moments later, she leaned back in the darkened theatre and gave herself up to the pure pleasure of Shakespeare well performed.

Next morning, Kate awoke with a bad headache. There were painkillers somewhere in the bathroom cabinet, if she could only find them. Making a misjudged grab she knocked over a bottle of shampoo. When she eventually emerged from the bathroom and pulled open the bedroom curtains she was in no mood for the sight which met her eyes.

Billows of mist were flinging a snowy tablecloth over Table Mountain, the sure sign of an impending south-easterly. There would be days of wind and rain, and after the long winter, she was tired of wind and rain. She padded into the kitchen for a cup of coffee and debated how much longer she could put off ringing her parents to inform them that there was no longer any prospective son-in-law.

With some surprise, she realised she was more concerned for them than for herself, but then, she wasn't thinking particularly straight this morning, which must account for the fact that every time she closed her eyes all she could see was the face of that disturbing man in the beach carpark.

The moment she heard her mother's calm voice over the telephone, Kate made her decision. 'I'm coming home.'

'How lovely, dear. You mean, for a brief holiday?'

'No. I've decided to leave Cape Town. You see, James and I have parted company, permanently.'

When her mother spoke she didn't sound unduly surprised.

'I see. Are you sure?'

'Absolutely. There is no way I could marry him now. Do you mind?'

'My dear, it's your happiness that counts. Want to tell me about it?'

'Not just yet.'

'Right, then. We'll be waiting for you, love.'

Within a week, Kate's car was nosing its way through the early-morning traffic, loaded to the hilt. Kate journeyed north towards the beautiful Hottentot's Holland Mountains which heralded the gateway into the interior, marking her long trek from the west coast of South Africa to the east. It had not taken her long to pack up, and Pippa's cousin had been only too pleased to take over the apartment, pot plants and all.

It was early September and everywhere the Cape spring was in evidence. Even the endless vineyards beside the highway were bursting with green. Kate wound down the window and sniffed the air with pleasure.

The sun had disappeared by the time

she pulled into the carpark of a small hotel where she hoped to secure a room for the night. How desperately she needed a shower to ease her cramped muscles, together with a good meal and glass of wine. Locking the car, she slung her overnight bag over one shoulder and wearily entered the foyer.

'It will be a pleasure, sir,' the reception clerk was saying. 'We have been expecting you. You've travelled up from Cape Town today? A long ride.'

He passed a key to the tall man in front of the desk.

'Indeed it is.'

Kate stared in disbelief at the figure in front of her. His was the sort of deep, velvet voice one could hardly forget. The beachcomber!

'Will the little lady be dining with you as well, sir?' the clerk asked.

Kate's eyes widened. So there was a female companion?

'No. A bowl of soup and some fruit should do, in about ten minutes.'

'I'll see to it,' the clerk promised.

'Would you like an early-morning call?'

'Five-thirty. I should like to make an early start.'

Kate smirked. No lie-in for the little woman! Up with the sun! Life with this man was undoubtedly one merry spin.

The man turned around, his eyes narrowing in sudden wary recognition. His eyes weren't silver as she'd supposed, but startlingly blue in a tanned face, a testimony to the fact that he was definitely an outdoor type.

'Will you take the second sitting for dinner, sir?' the clerk enquired.

He replied in the affirmative without removing his eyes from Kate's face. Kate blushed. She was aware of her crumpled appearance.

'I dress for comfort when I'm travelling,' she told him indignantly, 'and not in order to impress people.'

'Thank you for informing me,' he replied gravely.

Kate went up to the desk.

'A room for the night, please. And the first sitting for dinner, please.'

She dined later with relish, having eaten little all day except fruit. To round off the excellent meal, she chose a delightful crème caramel. She savoured another spoonful and glanced up, then choked.

He was standing in the doorway, pinning her once more with that direct gaze. Hurriedly she finished her coffee and left the dining-room.

Kate took another leisurely shower, put on her short, cotton nightdress and turned out the bedroom light before wandering out on to the small balcony. With a sigh of contentment she realised she would soon be home.

'Vicky?'

The words were no more than a whisper. Kate froze.

'Vicky, are you asleep?'

His voice came from inside her bedroom! He had obviously wandered into the wrong room! Silently Kate berated herself for her carelessness. How could she have been so stupid as to leave the door unlocked? She kept very still and peered into the room, hoping that he would quickly realise his mistake and leave. She was wrong. He went across to the bed, stared uncomprehendingly at its emptiness and snapped on the lamp.

'Vicky! What are you playing at?'

He strode towards the adjoining bathroom which naturally enough was vacant. With an oath, he spun around, discovered the balcony door was open, and leaped for it. To his amazement, he collided with Kate.

'You!'

'Yes, me,' Kate exclaimed.

'Where is Vicky?'

Kate eyed him coldly.

'How should I know? She's not here, as you can see.'

For a large man, he moved fast, grabbing her by the shoulders.

'What have you done with her?'

The savagery in his voice frightened her.

'I don't know what you're talking about. Now, please, get out!'

The man was unhinged, she thought wildly. The door was ajar. If she could just make a dash for it. But he had guessed her thoughts, and strode to the door and locked it, deliberately dropping the key into the pocket of his dinner jacket.

'Not until I get what I want,' he informed her grimly. 'You will now tell me what you have done with Victoria. You and my good friend, Felicia!'

Kate stood in stunned amazement. She swallowed nervously.

'Look,' she reasoned, 'I haven't the slightest idea what you're on about.'

'No? Then allow me to jog your memory. You were at the Nico Malan Theatre on Friday evening. You needn't bother to deny it, I saw you.'

'Yes,' Kate said, genuinely puzzled.

'Your accomplice went backstage, did she not? Anyone can see you're in it up to your pretty, little neck, and I'd give anything to strangle it right now!'

He made an abrupt move towards

her. Anger came to Kate's defence.

'Keep your filthy hands off me,' she shrilled, reaching for the telephone next to her bed, but a large hand clamped her wrist painfully.

'Oh, no, you don't! You will come clean with me, so save your breath. I want a satisfactory answer, and I have all night in which to get one.'

'I have nothing to tell you!'

'We'll start at the beginning, shall we? Vicky was in this room only half an hour ago. She was told not to open the door, an instruction with which she failed to comply. I return from dinner only to find she has disappeared.'

'I'm not surprised,' Kate jibed.

What an insufferable husband he must make!

'Who put you up to all this?' he insisted. 'Felicia, right?'

'Wrong!'

Kate had had enough.

'Get out of this room now, or I'll scream, do you hear me? I've no idea what you are talking about! You're

15

making a big mistake.'

'I am? Supposing you enlighten me, then.'

His face, now only inches from her own, looked murderous.

'Be warned that if anything happens to jeopardise either Vicky's safety or happiness, the pair of you will live to regret it.'

He released her abruptly.

'You are the weirdest person I've ever met,' Kate stormed. 'You barge into my room with some crazy story about your missing wife. Don't think you'll get away with this! I can even find it in me to feel sorry for her, with a husband like you. I have not, repeat not, spirited away your unfortunate spouse, with or without the assistance of this so-called Felicia, do you understand? Would you leave my room, now, please?'

He went very still.

'Wife? Did you say wife?'

'Yes,' Kate spat, flinging herself towards the door, 'this Victoria person. Now my key, if you please!'

The man was looking at her strangely.

'Er, key?' he said, sounding dazed.

'Yes, key, as in door. My door! This is my bed, my balcony, my room, and I would thank you to leave it, now!'

Slowly he drew two sets of keys from his jacket pocket and stared at them uncomprehendingly. Then he strode to the door, unlocked it and flung it open in order to compare the number on the outside with the keys in his hand. He muttered something under his breath, his face turning red.

'Allow me to apologise, Miss . . . er . . . my mistake. This does indeed appear to be your room and not Victoria's.'

The words trailed off as Kate snatched her key from him. She slammed the door behind him and leaned against it in order to take the weight off her suddenly trembling legs. Hopefully, she'd now seen the last of him . . .

2

By the time Kate reached her parent's home, she was tired of all the driving. It lay in a forested mist belt near the Umvoti River, farming country where timber, maize and cattle flourished. She drove through the centre of Bothatown and headed for the suburbs, eventually nosing her way through tall pillars flanking the gateway of her parents' home.

'Kate!' Mrs Howard cried as she embraced her daughter warmly and scanned her face. 'You've lost a little weight. We'll have to fatten you up.'

Kate smiled.

'What's for dinner, then?'

'The fatted calf, literally. Veal cutlets with that spicy crumbed coating you like and the new, homegrown carrots your father's so proud of.'

'And for afters?'

Her mother's glance was loving.

'Crêpes, what else, with lashings of cream and cinnamon!' Are you tired?

'Not a bit, now I'm home. Where's Dad?'

Kate's father was a man of few words.

'Hrrmph!' he said after dinner as they sat by a fire which had been lit to combat the early spring chill, and Kate had mentioned briefly that her husband-to-be had decided against marriage to his daughter.

The manner in which Bill Howard delivered this pronouncement was exceedingly eloquent. His daughter grinned.

'You mean,' she guessed correctly, 'that the man who refuses your daughter in marriage needs his head examined?'

Her father permitted himself a small smile.

'Something like that.'

'Thanks, Dad! I needed that vote of confidence. I intend putting my life back in order as soon as possible, too.'

'That's my girl.'

'What do you intend to do, work-wise?' Mary Howard asked.

'Haven't given it much thought,' Kate replied. 'I can't go back teaching until next year, can I? There's only one term left in the school year. I gave up my job last term to prepare for the wedding and do a bit of decorating. James didn't want me to work once we were married, so I'd sort of kissed my career goodbye.'

'I've been giving the matter some thought, Kate. Never fear when mother is near,' Mary Howard intoned with a twinkle. 'You must feel free to refuse, of course, but I thought it such an excellent opportunity. I mean, it would give your career a push in the right direction.'

'What would, Mother?'

'How would you like to be the principal of Happy Days Nursery School?'

'Principal?' Kate exclaimed in disbelief.

'Well, temporary acting principal,

actually. I was chatting to Mrs Rattray in the hairdresser's just after you phoned. She has to go into hospital briefly and has been putting it off because she can't get one term's replacement. Everyone she's interviewed seems to want something more permanent, so I said I'd speak to you. It's only for one term, after all.'

'But I've no experience of nursery schools. I'm primary trained.'

'Pooh! Once a teacher, always a teacher. You'll soon learn the ropes. It shouldn't take you long to find your feet. Anyway, Mrs Rattray seemed to think you were perfectly well enough qualified. What do you think?'

'Well, it'll be a challenge.'

By the end of the week, Kate's mother was surveying her with secret satisfaction. Good food, solid parental support and walks with Toby, the dog, had done wonders. Kate no longer had dark rings under her eyes but in their hazel depths a certain sadness still lurked. The loss was still new, Mrs Howard told herself judiciously, and Kate must be allowed to grieve.

'I went to see Mrs Rattray today,' Kate announced while they were having afternoon tea. 'She's given me a contract until the end of the year.'

'Darling, that's wonderful! When do you begin?'

'School goes back in a week. I'll have to find somewhere nearby to live.'

'You are welcome to stay here, you know,' Mary Howard said.

'Thanks, Mum, but I've been independent for so long now, it wouldn't feel right. Can I borrow some furniture until I'm established, though?'

'Of course, dear, but what will you do when this job runs out? There is always a place for you in the business.'

'I know.'

As a student, she'd often helped out and enjoyed it, but teaching was her first love. Besides, her father was a jeweller and if she worked for him she'd have to think about diamonds all day.

Not always a girl's best friend, she'd discovered.

On her first morning, Kate parked outside the school, situated on two acres in a busy suburb. After recent refurbishment, it could accommodate almost ninety children. It was also, she noticed, securely fenced. Child abductions had been known to occur even in a place like this. No money had been spared to make the school one she was proud to be in charge of.

With a pang, Kate remembered the hopes she'd had of happy games with their own children on the lawn of the white-washed cottage she and James had dreamed of. James would probably come to regret what he'd thrown away but by then it would be too late.

She locked the car and walked beneath the shade of the jacaranda trees lining the street. In the school grounds, bougainvillaea blazed a welcome so heartening she began to lose some of her nervousness.

The children were excited to see a

new face in Mrs Rattray's office but it took less than a week for the novelty to wear off and the school settled into the final term. By the end of the second week, Kate felt she'd been there for years.

'You have been most efficient, Pam,' she told her secretary. 'Thanks to you, I've had an easy transition.'

Pam Shaw flushed with pleasure.

'Only doing what I'm paid to do, Kate. You're rather a tonic to have around, you know. New ideas, and it's . . . a man!'

Kate started guiltily.

'I beg your pardon?'

'I said,' Pam reiterated, 'a man! There's a man outside.'

Kate stared. What on earth was Pam on about?

'Do take a look,' Pam begged. 'See that dark grey car next to the kerb, with the tree in front of it? Well, he's skulking behind the tree.'

'Now look here, Pam — '

'Kate, please!'

Pam was genuinely troubled.

'Believe me, I'm not joking. I noticed him earlier in the day, and last year, a child went missing from a school near here. Ever since then, we've been particularly careful, on Mrs Rattray's orders.'

'I see.'

Kate decided to take a look. The street was almost empty. Only one gentleman appeared to be ignoring the fierceness of the sun, and at that moment he was stepping from the shade of a tree as though on cue, turning to approach a small girl playing near the fence.

'There!' Pam hissed. 'What did I tell you?'

Kate stiffened. There was something disconcertingly familiar about the man as he bent down to hear what the child was saying. The little girl pointed towards the school building and ran off to play.

Kate wasn't about to spook at ghosts, however, and did her best to ignore it.

Pam could surely be pacified with a little reasoning.

'Technically, he's done nothing wrong, Pam. It seems a bit drastic to summon the police. After all, he may simply be an innocent bystander, seeking shade on a hot day. Or perhaps he asked the child for directions.'

'Innocent bystander, my foot!' Pam said crossly. 'He's very definitely suspect. What ordinary citizen would skulk on the sidewalk all morning, peering at children through the trees? What ordinary person would do that, unless he has some kind of a problem?'

'All morning, did you say?'

'Well, nearly all morning. For all we know he'll be chatting up the gardener next, finding out all about our security arrangements.'

She gave a sudden shriek.

'Look! He's climbing our fence!'

True, Kate thought, he was holding on to the mesh with both hands as though testing its strength, and looking up as though to gauge its height.

'It is a bit strange, I will admit.'

'I agree with you, Pam. It's an odd way to behave. There's no harm in having him investigated.'

Within minutes of her phone call, excited cries arose from the garden. Soon the entire school had rushed out to watch admiringly as the police captain climbed from his yellow patrol car with its flashing blue light, a fierce-looking dog barking excitedly behind a grid in the rear section.

The officer approached the sidewalk, exchanged a few patently humorous remarks with the stranger, heartily shook his hand and climbed back into the patrol car. Kate, watching from the window, was speechless.

'Well! You'd have thought they were old friends. That policeman could at least have consulted me before disappearing. I have a good mind to go down and confront the man myself!'

'No need,' her secretary said grimly. 'I do believe he has the same idea. He's marching up the front path, Kate, and by the look on his face an army wouldn't keep him out!'

'But he can't do that,' Kate said indignantly. 'The gate is locked! He ought to be ringing the gate-bell. Even the parents have to do that if they arrive once school is underway.'

'Too late, dear. It seems he has already negotiated that obstacle by climbing over. The man's a total weirdo.'

By now, Kate was too angry to stand and speculate about the figure striding up the path towards the colonnaded veranda. She marched from the office like a lioness in defence of her young. Of all the nerve!

For once, the hallway, brilliant with child art, gave her no pleasure. Her sandaled feet tapped furiously on the polished floor and to make things worse she stubbed her toe on a potted palm near the front door. The shrill of the doorbell rang out. Kate saw red.

'Do you mind?'

She flung open the door.

'This is a school, for pity's sake, not the county jail.'

Her eyes widened incredulously.

'Is that so?' the stranger from the beach drawled, his large shoulder propping up the door frame. 'You could have fooled me.'

'You again! What do you want this time?'

He appeared in no hurry to reply, his eyes fixed on her face in a manner which left her in no doubt that she had his full, angry attention. Kate held on to her temper.

'State your business, please. What exactly do you want?'

'Not you,' he replied insolently, 'so you can relax. No, I've bigger fish to fry. Take me to the person who runs this establishment, although why I don't just try another school beats me, since I am completely unable to gain access via any of the normally accepted channels.'

He continued to glare.

'For example, I telephoned here yesterday afternoon but, alas, you do not deign to answer such modern devices. Consequently I arrive in person this morning only to discover to my utter astonishment that you've all barricaded yourselves in. Further, whilst standing in total perplexity upon the sidewalk trying to seek help from one of your young inmates, I am accosted by an officer of the law. Fortunately, said officer and I go back a long way so I am not exactly constrained to establish my credentials. I then discover that there is but one option left — to climb over the gate, not to mention having to hammer down the front door!

'Would you be so good as to enlighten me, please? Is this the way you treat all prospective parents? If it is, your public relations are woefully lacking!'

3

Kate paled. 'Prospective parent?' she gasped in disbelief as he stood in front of her.

'Providing you manage to stay in business long enough, that is. Take me to your head teacher, please!'

It wasn't often she misjudged a situation this badly. The man was furious, and rightly so. He was muttering something extremely uncomplimentary under his breath and she had no wish to know what it was.

'Give me strength! I see they employ fools here, into the bargain. Let me spell it out, lady. Take — me — ' he repeated as though to a small child.

Kate recovered swiftly.

'There is no need to be offensive, Mr — '

'Watson,' he clipped. 'Peter Watson.'

'I apologise for any inconvenience

you've experienced, Mr Watson. There seems to have been a slight misunderstanding. May I explain that the reason your call was not answered yesterday is a simple one. The school closes at noon and — '

'Forget it.'

'And please be informed for future reference, Mr Watson, that there is a perfectly good bell on the gate for use once school is in progress. There was absolutely no need to break and enter!'

A glimmer of amusement which appeared in the blue eyes was quickly extinguished.

'I see. Thank you for clearing that up. However, now that I've managed to get this far, I would like to interview the principal, a Miss Kathryn Howard.'

'That is correct.'

Kate turned and marched him down the passage to her office.

'Please be seated.'

She indicated a chair and opened a drawer of her desk to extract a form.

'Am I to understand that you wish to

make application for your child to enter this nursery school, Mr Watson? If so, you may complete this form.'

'I'll not be fobbed off this easily, lady. I asked to see Miss Howard and Miss Howard I will see, not someone hardly out of the nursery herself.'

Kate had the distinct urge to feed the man to the lions, but a prospective parent had to be treated with civility, if she could muster any.

'I do regret that you take me for a half-wit, Mr Watson,' she told him sweetly, 'but let me hasten to assure you that I am both professionally qualified and personally able to run this school, a fact you will simply have to take my word for. I am Kate Howard.'

'You're the principal?' he asked in open-mouthed astonishment.

It was obvious he was having difficulty in digesting this unpalatable fact as his narrowed eyes flicked over her in lightning reassessment.

'I see. In that case, shall we do business?'

He reached for the form, and sat down opposite her.

'It seems yet again I owe you an apology, Miss Howard. In my day, schoolma'ams looked nothing like you. You don't look a day over twenty.'

'I assure you, I'm twenty-four, not that my precise age has any relevance whatever to this interview.'

He disagreed.

'Any prospective parent has every right to ensure that their child will be in responsible, adult hands. But yes, twenty-four is an estimable age.'

He was laughing at her behind that inscrutable gaze and she determined to get rid of him as soon as possible.

'Sign here, please.'

She indicated with her left hand and saw his eyes rest on the pale mark still obvious on her third finger.

'What exactly did he do to you, Miss Howard?'

'I beg your pardon?'

'The man who put that look in your lovely eyes.'

'It is hardly any of your business! Any further questions?'

'Yes. What are you afraid of?'

He was writing quickly, his tone casual.

'I'm not afraid of anything, Mr Watson. I take it that your daughter . . .'

'Vicky.'

Her eyes widened. So Victoria wasn't the name of his wife but his daughter — the 'little lady' he had been so paranoid about at the hotel!

'I take it she has had the usual inoculations.'

It was his turn to look blank.

'What inoculations?'

'Diphtheria, tetanus, whooping cough,' Kate said hiding her impatience. 'Perhaps you could ask your wife, Mr Watson, and let me know.'

'Wife?' His direct gaze faltered as he spoke. 'I see.'

'I suggest that you take the health form home for Victoria's mother who will doubtless know her health record. You can return it by post. Now, I shall see you out.'

Mr Watson's good humour disappeared.

'Victoria's mother,' he snapped, 'will be signing nothing. Is that clear? I am responsible for the child and whatever you need will be signed by me.'

'If you cannot comply with our requirements, I have no option but to refuse your child entry.'

Mr Watson jumped up.

'I will try to ascertain if Victoria has been suitably inoculated. All I can do meantime is appeal to you to allow the child to enrol.'

It was quite obviously the nearest thing to a plea he could bring himself to make.

'In that case, I am prepared to put the child's name on our list but I will require that information as soon as possible.'

He hesitated.

'Perhaps I ought to explain that I'm a busy man and I've not had much experience with young children.'

It was an odd confession for a man

whose child was already four years old, and he seemed to realise it. There was a bleakness in his eyes.

'I haven't had much to do with her before now. I daresay I could leave her to play about the farm all day but that would not be in her best interests. Vicky has not had much of a life until now and I'm anxious to make it up to her. I would be in your debt if she could begin as soon as possible.'

Kate was forced to disappoint him.

'I had no idea you were expecting immediate admission, Mr Watson. I'm afraid that's impossible as we've no vacancies at present. I imagined this application was only for next year. Even then, it would have to be processed before a decision could be taken.'

She walked to the door.

'Would you be good enough to post us those completed forms? We will then notify you in due course.'

'Are you saying that you won't take the child from Monday?'

Kate took a deep breath. Didn't the

man have any idea of what was entailed in running a school this size? Obviously not!

'Perhaps I should enlighten you, Mr Watson. We have nearly one hundred children and they are divided into three groups according to age. There are a certain number of places in each group and each one has a waiting list. There is absolutely no way I could place your child's name on top of the list before the others. Surely you can see that? The usual procedure — '

'I am not concerned with usual procedure. As far as I am concerned, Vicky begins school on Monday and if there is no vacancy at present, you will create one. Is that clear?'

Kate's patience finally snapped.

'No, it is not! I have already taken more than enough of your bulldozing, Mr Watson. When will you realise that you cannot simply threaten and manipulate in order to get what you want? I have a school to run and I will not depart from usual procedure! You may see yourself out. Good day.'

'Wait.'

Something in his voice made her turn around.

'I had no wish to manipulate you, Miss Howard. Surely you can recognise desperation when you see it. I would be grateful if you were to reconsider.'

'I'm afraid I can't.'

He gave her a long, grim stare.

'Abduction. Do you know what that means?'

'Of course I do.'

'Desperate situations require desperate measures. That, Miss Howard, is what I have just done with Vicky — abducted her.'

Kate went cold. Pam had been right, the man was a weirdo.

'I'll send for some coffee,' she suggested, picking up the telephone.

She reached for her notepad, intending to pass Pam a surreptitious message when she came in. The police must be informed. This time Mr Watson would not get away. All she had to do in the meantime was keep him talking. In a few hours, those massive shoulders would be behind bars.

'I had to do it, you know,' he was continuing. 'I was within my rights.'

'Surely that's a contradiction in terms?'

She tried to keep her voice matter-of-fact. Why was Pam taking so long?

'No. In this case I happen also to be the child's legal guardian.'

He's lying, Kate thought. You didn't have to steal what is legally yours.

'Let me explain,' he went on. 'I was given custody of Vicky only three weeks ago after a long and costly wrangle, and an ugly one. I have no wish ever to repeat such a thing.'

'What of the child's mother?' Kate prompted.

'By statute, custody of a child under the age of sixteen is regulated by the court in the best interests of the child. Vicky's mother has been denied all access, which fact speaks for itself. Does that make it clear? Do you understand now why I will not permit the woman to sign those forms, let alone come anywhere near that child?'

'Whatever your personal circumstances, Mr Watson, they do not alter the fact that there is no vacancy at Happy Days. I'm sorry.'

'I realise that. I am asking you to create one.'

'Why should I do that for one child and not another?'

'Because I'm begging you to.'

'It is highly irregular.'

'Yes. Let me enlighten you further, because this is no ordinary child, loved and cared for. The truth is, I rescued her from an intolerable situation of abuse and neglect. Her mother was for some unaccountable reason refusing to give her up, not, I suspect, from any noble motives. I travelled to Cape Town and cultivated the friendship of one of Felicia's female cronies in the hope of finding out where she was hiding the child. It worked.'

He continued grimly, 'When I realised

that Vicky was at home alone, I simply broke in and abducted her. She is now here with me, where she belongs, and God help that woman if she ever comes near us again. If she does,' he rasped, 'I personally will tear her limb from limb.'

Pam arrived at last with the coffee, her eyes round.

'Everything OK?' she mouthed behind Mr Watson's back.

Kate nodded reassuringly and waited for the door to close. If he was telling the truth then it would not behove her to take the matter further, would it? She had a sneaking sympathy for him, and the child deserved every chance to be happy.

'Will you reconsider?' he persisted quietly. 'In your position you are entitled to do as you please but I would like to point out that your school has the best security arrangements in town. I've checked them out. Vicky has had more disappointments than you or I have had Sunday dinners, and I promised her she could start school on

Monday, never thinking . . . '

He broke off helplessly and Kate thought quickly.

'It would seem that yours is indeed an unusual situation, Mr Watson. I like to weigh each case on its merits, and our policy here is to regard the child's needs as our primary concern.'

She reached for a buff folder on the desk.

'The four-year-old group is already fully subscribed, but I will make a special concession. I'll ask the teacher concerned to simply make a place because there are not many more weeks left in the school year and I'm reasonably sure she'll comply. Vicky may begin on Monday.'

Kate looked up to surprise the immense relief in his eyes.

'Thank you. I'll not forget this.'

At the door, he paused, obviously at a loss.

'Er . . . what shall she wear?'

'Anything comfortable and not too smart. Jeans and T-shirt should do.'

'Right. One last thing.' The steely eyes held hers like a magnet. 'I will be holding you personally responsible for that child's safety, Miss Howard. Is that understood?'

'You need have no cause for concern, Mr Watson. We will take every care with her, as we do with all of our charges.'

A sudden smile formed attractive creases down his cheeks, lighting his eyes in a way she had not noticed before. What a strange man he was, compelling yet infuriating; having by turns an air of commanding reassurance or touching vulnerability, especially when it came to a small girl by the name of Victoria.

It was Sunday evening and guileless blue eyes peered at Kate from the safety of the sofa. The move to her new apartment had gone smoothly enough the previous day and now she contemplated the latest addition to the household. Piteous mewing had compelled her to investigate the hedge around her garden where she'd found him, and within minutes Sebastian was warmly ensconced, licking the milk from his tiny whiskers.

Those vivid eyes reminded her of another pair, equally irresistible. Kate shook her head. What was she thinking of? Mr Watson was a parent, for goodness' sake. To regard him in another other light was not only unthinkable, but totally unprofessional.

She had to admit to a certain curiosity about his past. What had he meant by 'intolerable situations' and 'disappointments'? Happy Days would just have to live up to its name for the child and provide a stable, fulfilling environment for her as it did for all the others. The prospect of a child hurting in any way produced a fierce protectiveness in Kate. She resolved to waste no time in befriending Vicky and knew without conceit that she was good at handling difficult children. By her reckoning, this one should be a brat.

'Good morning.'

Vicky Watson greeted Kate shyly but with perfect politeness. Her next and obviously rehearsed words came out in a rush.

'Thank you for letting me come to your school.'

Kate was taken aback. She took the child's hand and scanned the expressionless face, noting the dark eyes almost too large for the perfect oval face, which gazed back with a touch of apprehension in their depths. Vicky had the air of being perpetually braced against life and no four-year-old, Kate thought fiercely, should be required to bear that kind of burden.

'It's a pleasure to have you, Vicky,' she responded warmly. 'We all have a great deal of fun here. Your teacher, Mrs Reddy, is waiting for you so we'll go and meet her. Miss Reddy looks after the children in the Blue Group, and I know she has something very exciting to show you all today.'

Vicky refused to budge. She flung herself into Mr Watson's arms and clung for a mute, terrified moment. Over her head his glance was helpless.

'Would you like to come with us, Mr Watson?' Kate responded smoothly. 'Then you can see where Vicky is so you'll know exactly where to fetch her at the end of the morning. Come along, Vicky, we'll show him your room. Did you know that Mrs Reddy keeps a hamster there? He's called Pumpkin and I'll tell you why.'

Kate chatted all the way to the Blue Area and paused just long enough to hear Vicky's fierce whisper.

'Don't forget to fetch me!'

'I'll be there, Vicky, that's a promise. I fetched you all the way from Cape Town, didn't I?' he replied.

With a smile, Mrs Reddy picked herself up from the floor where she'd been sitting with the children, engrossed in a puzzle.

'I'm Violet Reddy,' she introduced herself to Mr Watson, 'and this must be Vicky. What a pretty T-shirt that is. It's almost the same colour as mine!'

Vicky relaxed visibly and allowed herself to be drawn into an activity

47

threading bright scraps of wool through holes punched into card.

'I'll disappear while the going's good, shall I?' Mr Watson said quietly.

Kate nodded and when he had gone, she set out on her rounds to ensure that all the play areas were in readiness for the free-play period when the children left their group teachers and chose their own activities.

The Creative Room was a joy to behold with its many prepared activities, and soon it would be humming with happily-occupied children. In the Observation Room she noticed the books and puzzles which had been carefully chosen to support the week's theme, Black and White in Nature. Zebras, pandas and the like stared back at her and even the Fantasy Room held dressing-up clothes featuring spots and stripes of every description.

The day flew by and soon parents began to arrive for their offspring. As usual Kate stood at the door to greet them. Chatting busily, she noticed from the corner of her eye a tall, bush-jacketed figure striding by in his work clothes and her heart missed a beat.

Bothatown served a large, agricultural community and booted, khaki-clad males in bush hats were hardly an unusual sight. Why, then, should she be so affected? Hadn't she always shied away from so-called macho men with their much brawn and little brain? That was why she'd gone for someone like James in the first place, with his fine mind and gentle manner. Not that it had got her anywhere, she had to admit. So why was she standing like a schoolgirl watching Mr Watson's departing back, savouring the strain of his shoulders against the thin material of his khaki shirt?

Kate took a deep, steadying breath. This was no way for a school principal to act!

After school Kate met her mother in town for coffee. They ordered large slices of gateau and watched the shoppers stream past the window.

'How's school?' Kate's mother asked.

'Fine,' Kate replied then found herself telling her mother about Vicky.

'Watson did you say the name was? How strange. Last week I met up with an old school friend from Pietermaritzburg by the name of Elizabeth Watson. Wonder if there's any connection? She said her son was farming around these parts. Peter, I think she said his name was.'

Kate choked. Her mother's eyes sharpened. Something in Kate's expression made her decide not to pursue the subject. Thoughtfully she poured herself another cup of tea. There was no harm in having a cosy chat with Elizabeth at the next Women's Institute meeting, was there?

'Will you come to dinner soon, Kate? I'll let you know which evening suits your father. He's rather busy at present, gearing up for the Christmas trade. I keep telling him he should find a manager for the shop. It would take the pressure off.'

'Any evening would suit me, Mum. Not much social life at present.'

'Perhaps you should give your old friends a ring?'

'I might do that. I'm enjoying work but apart from that my life seems to be going nowhere at present.'

'You're doing fine, Kate. Give yourself time, love. You've made a start on picking up the pieces, and that's the main thing.'

'I s'pose so.'

Next morning, Vicky appeared, wearing a shy smile.

'Good morning, Miss Howard.'

Kate was touched that she'd remembered her name. The child was clean and tidy and someone had taken great pains with her hair.

'What a pretty ribbon, Vicky.'

She was rewarded by an even bigger smile.

'Albertina tied it for me.'

Who, Kate wondered, was Albertina. This time Vicky took leave of her father a little more confidently and went with Kate to find the plastic aprons. She spent most of the morning in the Creative Room producing a zebra picture with surprising talent.

On Friday morning, Mrs Reddy brought Kate some unwelcome news.

'Oh, dear, are you sure?' she said in astonishment.

'I know head lice when I see them. It's only Vicky who's infected.'

'I see. Well, she'll have to be promptly treated of course, or within days we could have a problem! Thanks, Violet.'

Kate went into the office and asked Pam Shaw to telephone Mr Watson.

'Tell him he'll have to remove Vicky until the condition is clear. It's standard procedure.'

Pam opened Vicky's file on the computer, located the telephone number and made the call. Kate went into her office to attack the pile of paperwork on her desk. Hopefully there would be no more interruptions. Within minutes, however, the telephone shrilled at her elbow and Pam informed her that Mr

Watson was on the line.

'How can I help you, Mr Watson?'

'For a start you can tell me just what kind of an operation you are running.'

'I beg your pardon?'

'When last did you people have a proper health inspection? You have the effrontery, Miss Howard, to inform me I must remove my child until further notice. What's your problem?'

'One moment, Mr Watson.'

'Vicky has contracted this condition after only one week at your school. With the kind of fees you charge, I must say I think you have a nerve.'

Kate held on to her temper. He was the one who had the nerve, but if there was one thing experience had taught her it was how to handle overactive parents.

'You have every right to be annoyed, Mr Watson, and if it were my child I'd feel the same,' she said sweetly.

'Now you're talking.'

'However, I'm very much afraid that you have the incorrect information.

Vicky is the only child in the entire school who is infected. She arrived with head lice, and by the look of things, she must have had them for weeks.'

'That's impossible,' he exploded angrily.

'It's true. In everyone's interests she will have to be isolated until the treatment has been successful. It is nothing to be concerned about. A fairly common occurrence.'

'Treatment?' he sounded bewildered. 'What treatment?'

She explained the details politely and rang off.

Kate tried to concentrate on the year-end reports but Vicky's problem kept surfacing. With a sigh she replaced her files and went to the first-aid box. Sure enough, there was a spare bottle of special shampoo. She may as well offer to treat the child herself to ensure the operation was a success and Vicky could return to school as soon as possible. How could one possibly trust Mr Watson to do the job properly when it was so painfully obvious the man hadn't a clue? She found Vicky in the Creative Room and took her into the office.

'What pretty hair you have, Vicky. Would you like me to wash it for you with some special shampoo I have?'

'Now?' the child queried.

'Why not? Would you like that?'

'We like,' came a deep voice from the doorway, 'don't we, Vicky?'

Kate spun around as Vicky ran to Mr Watson.

'I don't want to get my hair washed at school,' she wailed.

'No? Why not, princess?'

'The others don't get theirs washed at school. I don't have to, do I?'

'Of course not. I have a better idea. Let's invite Miss Howard to Hazelburn this afternoon for tea, and if you feel like it later on, perhaps she will give you a pretty hairdo in your own bathroom. Will that do?'

His eyes met Kate's their expression veiled.

'Would you come out to Hazelburn this afternoon, Miss Howard?'

Kate was about to refuse when she caught sight of Vicky's face, alive with anticipation. She sighed.

'It's highly irregular but yes, I'll come.'

'Excellent. We'll expect you at three. Let me give you some directions.'

A moment later, Mr Watson took Vicky by the hand.

'Come along, Vicky.' He grinned. 'I hope you can bake a cake because I certainly can't!'

Having installed the child safely in the car he pulled into the traffic unaware of the yellow sports car parked across the street. The elegant red-head behind the wheel stared after him from behind designer sunglasses, a satisfied smile on her carefully-outlined lips.

It was just as she'd thought — he had the child with him! She would telephone Cape Town this evening.

4

The sign said clearly, Hazelburn. Behind it, hills clawed the distant sky above irrigated fields stretching for miles under a hot sun. A dusty track wound around the hill past maize, vegetables and kikuyu pastures.

Kate's car bounced along like a ride at a fun fair, leaving behind it a cloud of red earth. Mr Watson really ought to do something about the state of his road, Kate thought in irritation. Around a corner, a white-washed homestead appeared with its equally neat cluster of satellite buildings rising from acres of emerald lawn. Splashes of pink and scarlet bougainvillaea against the veranda vied with bright spring flowers in the borders. As her car stopped, two Alsatians sprang up noisily to investigate her arrival. Mr Watson strode from the house, called them off and politely opened her car door.

'You found us easily enough?'

Kate nodded.

'Where's Vicky?'

'This way.'

She followed him to where Vicky was playing and then he took them to the bathroom. An hour later, Vicky emerged with short, shining hair. Rather a lot had been cut off but at least it was trouble free.

'A woman of many talents, Miss Howard?' Mr Watson commented.

'Vicky has such lovely hair,' Kate said, 'that one wonders how it could have been so neglected.'

She bit back the words.

'Oh! I'm sorry, I didn't mean to be rude.'

'Vicky, would you ask Albertina to bring in the tea, please?'

Obediently Vicky left.

'Her mother simply did not care,' Mr Watson continued. 'No maternal instincts whatever. She was totally self-absorbed. By the time I'd located

Vicky in Cape Town she hadn't eaten a decent meal for two days. Two days!' His eyes were murderous. 'She was also unwashed, alone and frightened. And to think I imagined her in good hands!'

At last Kate understood the reason for his dark thoughts on the shore the day she'd first seen him. Shock . . . anger . . . guilt.

'A friend discovered Vicky sleeping on the floor in a theatre dressing-room while her mother was away cavorting with the latest lover in a luxury apartment on the seafront. When I discovered that, I hired the best lawyer. It was worth every cent because I now have Vicky. Felicia,' he said harshly, 'is certainly a very good actress. She had us all fooled.'

'I thought she was quite wonderful in 'Macbeth'.'

'Oh, she was wonderful, all right, the great Felicia Watson.'

'Your wife?'

'Correction, my erstwhile and erring fiancée. When she met my brother she dropped me like I had the plague when it became apparent he was richer than I was and he stood to inherit the farm. She married him, poor besotted fool that he was. Felicia Watson is my late brother's wife.'

Albertina greeted Kate smilingly as she wheeled in the tea trolley.

'Shall I pour, Mr Watson?' Kate offered.

'If you would.'

Proudly, Vicky bore in an enormous chocolate masterpiece.

'Nobody's allowed to cut it,' she instructed, 'except Miss Howard. Albertina says.'

'Is that so?' Mr Watson said, hiding a smile.

Vicky breathed carefully as she set the cake down and looked at Kate expectantly, unaware that her principal was having difficulty in swallowing. Enormous importance was being attached to this visit, not to mention the way in which the cake had been concocted at such short notice.

'I'd be delighted, Vicky.'

'You have no option,' Mr Watson commented dryly. 'Albertina's word is law in this household and I have no say in these matters at all.'

Kate hid a smile.

'It's a beautiful cake, Vicky'

After tea, Vicky snuggled up to Kate on the sofa.

'Would you like to see Bobby?' she ventured.

'Who is Bobby?'

'Beauty's calf. He was born last night, and Uncle Peter stayed awake the whole night to help her.'

It was the first time Kate had heard him referred to as Uncle Peter, bearing out the now-revealed relationship.

'I'd like that, Vicky, and then I'm afraid I will have to leave. Sebastian will be waiting for his dinner.'

Mr Watson shot her an intent look.

'The boyfriend?'

'The man in my life,' Kate agreed, 'but he happens to be a kitten and he gets very hungry by six o'clock.'

Vicky digested this thoughtfully.

'Just like Uncle Peter,' she said.

'Oh, absolutely, I have a very good appetite,' he agreed outrageously. 'It must be my Latin blood. I had an Italian grandmother, you know.'

'Really? I didn't realise that.'

'Why should you? Anyway, as I have been telling you, appearances can be deceptive.'

Kate studied his face.

'Oh, I can see it now: tanned complexion, straight nose, proud head, even the sensuous mouth, when you're not angry.'

'Sensuous,' he mocked. 'Appealing to the senses, I think that means.'

'But not to mine,' she retorted. 'I really must go. Thank you for the tea.'

'Do you live up to your description, Kate?' he asked blandly.

'What do you mean?'

' 'Kate',' he quoted from 'The Taming Of The Shrew.' ' 'Like the hazel-twig, is straight and slender: and as brown in hue, as hazelnuts, and sweeter than the kernels . . . ''

Next morning, Kate glanced at herself in the small mirror in her office. Hazelnuts, indeed! To be honest, what had really surprised her was that Peter Watson knew his Shakespeare. Farmers were supposed to be all brawn, weren't they?

She reached up and touched a glossy brown strand of fringe feathering her forehead above the perfect brows. Beneath them, calm hazel eyes were reflecting the golden light. A slight movement made her spin round, to see a redhead eyeing her coldly from the doorway. Her hair and clothing were immaculate, almost as though she had stepped from the pages of a glossy magazine, and her green eyes flicked over Kate.

'What did you say?' Kate said, caught offguard.

'I said, I will not be kept waiting while a nurserymaid preens herself!'

Kate took a deep breath to control her anger.

'Who are you and what exactly is it you want?'

'I have come to collect Victoria Watson, and I am in a hurry. That woman in the office next door refuses to fetch her.'

'Your name, please?'

'My name has nothing to do with it.'

'I am very much afraid that it has.'

'You are impertinent. I will see that you are reprimanded by the principal. Fetch her at once!'

'I am the principal, and I insist that you tell me your name.'

The brilliant eyes became little more than slits.

'Miss Imelda Barnard. You will doubtless have heard of me.'

'I'm afraid I haven't.'

'No? Well, I don't suppose you are exposed much to any culture in these parts. I am a close friend of Peter Watson.'

Pam was at the door, an outraged expression on her face.

'I'm sorry, Kate. I did explain to this lady that parents may not collect children before closing time without prior notice, but . . . '

'Thank you, Pam.'

Kate dismissed her with a smile and turned to Miss Barnard.

'We may not, for security reasons, allow children to be collected without a prior letter of consent from the parents or guardians.'

The woman was unimpressed.

'I am not about to concern myself with your petty rules and regulations. Fetch Victoria Watson immediately, if you please.'

Kate controlled her temper admirably.

'Our rules, Miss Barnard, are made in the interests of safety and even if I did have a letter from Mr Watson I would still require some form of identification from you. How do I know you are who you claim to be?'

'I have no such identification on me. I warn you, if you do not release the child immediately you will have Mr Watson to answer to.'

Kate decided to call her bluff. She reached for the telephone.

'Would you wait in my secretary's office while I telephone, please?'

Miss Barnard had no intention of complying. She merely draped herself over the chair in front of the desk and eyed Kate in smug satisfaction.

'Yes?' Albertina replied to Kate's call to Hazelburn.

'Is Mr Watson there, Albertina? This is Miss Howard.'

Miss Barnard's eyes narrowed. How did the principal of Happy Days come to be so familiar with the names of Peter's domestic staff? The woman was attractive enough, too. Quite stunning, in fact, with honey-coloured skin and those nut-brown looks. There was the possibility of competition here, and nothing, least of all this ill-dressed child-minder, must be allowed to destroy her carefully-laid plans.

'Watson here.' He sounded annoyed. 'What is it, Miss Howard?'

Like him, Kate wasted no words.

'Do I have your permission for a certain Miss Imelda Barnard to remove

Vicky from school?'

'For heaven's sake, you summon me from an urgent veterinary consultation just to ask that? The answer, Miss Howard, is yes! Is there some problem with that?'

'It's just that this is highly irregular. In future — '

'For your information, Miss Howard, I asked Imelda to collect Vicky on my behalf at twelve seeing that she would be coming out to Hazelburn for lunch and I thought to save myself the trip. It has obviously proved more convenient for her to call in earlier. I hope you have not annoyed her.'

'Oh, not at all, Mr Watson. It's quite the other way round. Your friend lacks even the rudiments of the social graces. As I was about to say,' she continued, her tone deceptively sweet, 'should you require your child early then please have the courtesy in future to inform the school in advance.'

Angrily she slammed down the receiver.

Marching into the garden to find Vicky, she was conscious of the smirking Miss Barnard and purposely left her to the mercies of a still irate Pam who ushered her into the foyer. Vicky was in the garden, playing with dough.

'Vicky, I must ask you to go and wash your hands now, please. Miss Barnard is here to take you home.'

Vicky looked alarmed.

'But I don't want to go with her. I don't like her. I want Uncle Peter.'

'He can't fetch you today because he's very busy. Come along. We had better not keep her waiting.'

'But I don't want to,' Vicky wailed. 'I don't like her!'

'I'll tell you what. Take this dough home.'

Hastily she gathered the few remaining pieces into a lump.

'You can feed Uncle Peter's doggies when you get home.'

Vicky went without further objection.

'We could make some ducks, too,'

she was heard telling a patently bored Miss Barnard who hurried her out of the door.

Vicky arrived at school the following morning accompanied by a uniformed driver who introduced himself as Alpheus, husband of Albertina. He handed Kate a large white envelope.

This is to inform you that my driver Alpheus will accompany Vicky to and from school in future, Mr Watson had written in bold letters. **I apologise for yesterday's inconvenience. Perhaps you will accept the enclosed as a peace offering?**

Wondering what to expect Kate lifted the lid of the cardboard box Vicky was excitedly offering her. Nestling on a bed of straw was a beautifully-modelled set of pink farm animals and in the centre holding pride of place was Vicky's own contribution, a vague replica of the calf, Bobby!

That evening, Kate flicked through her wardrobe, wondering what to wear. There was her mother's cooking to look forward to as well as the opportunity to meet her father's new business partner. She opted for a swirling, ocean-coloured skirt and teamed it with an off-shoulder peasant blouse. Its colour always reminded her of the Atlantic at Cape Point and with a small shock she realised she hadn't thought of James for days.

Her mother had been right, the new job had certainly kept her from brooding. On the other hand, what did it say for the strength of her love that she'd been able to forget him that easily? In order not to be late she took a shorter route than usual through the town. Her mind, however, wasn't quite on her driving, being occupied with a set of exquisite tiny pink animals in a cardboard box which she had put on display in the school foyer, and a certain Peter Watson also filled her thoughts.

He was the most attractive and intriguing man she had ever met. She would have to be very careful. She could easily fall for him, and that would never do. Too late, her heart informed her, beginning a tattoo of its own. Startled at the unexpected and unwelcome discovery, she felt the blood rush to her cheeks.

Her cheeks were still pink as she drew to a halt outside her parent's home where an unfamiliar blue Mercedes was parked on the drive.

'This is my new assistant, Grant Edwards,' her father introduced their guest. 'My daughter, Kathryn.'

Kate greeted Mr Edwards with interest. He was tall and fair, immaculate in a dark suit and pristine shirt. He returned her interest.

'I've heard all about you, Kathryn.'

'Call me Kate. Everyone does.'

She kissed her mother and noted her suspiciously bland expression. Realisation dawned. Dear mother was matchmaking! Kate chose the sofa, accepted a glass of wine and decided on a safe topic of conversation.

'How long have you worked in the

jewellery business, Grant?'

It was a mistake. Flattered by her attention, he droned on with an ego as big as the Empire State Building!

Nice little filly, he was thinking. Knows how to dress.

'Now that your father has realised my calibre,' he droned on, 'there's a possible partnership ... hope to expand the business ... '

Kate resigned herself to a long, boring evening.

During the meal, she was forced to acknowledge that Grant Edwards' expertise would undoubtedly be an asset to her father, but unlike her parents she failed to appreciate the fascinating merits of Brazilian amethysts over African AA, or was it the other way round? Her mother's cooking was the only redeeming feature of the whole evening.

'Dad,' she said to change the subject, 'how's the ankle? That fall you had was not to be taken lightly, was it?'

'I wanted to speak to you about that,

Kate. Could you help out in the business tomorrow morning while I have an X-ray? I'm sure Grant would be grateful for your help.'

Kate arrived early the following morning and sought out Grant Edwards.

'Anything specific you'd like me to do, Grant? I could take the front counter with Margo, if you like.'

Grant cast an appreciative eye over her cream watered silk outfit and single strand of pearls, in no apparent hurry to send her off.

'Do you mind if I say that you have excellent taste, Kate? One thing, though. I would appreciate it if you would not address me as Grant while at work. The other staff, you know.'

'Certainly, Mr Edwards. It's best not to mix business with pleasure.'

'Exactly. Perhaps you would take the front counter?'

He couldn't believe his luck. The boss's daughter was the best thing since sliced bread. Sophisticated, biddable, knew her place. He would waste no time. He would take her out to dinner as soon as could be arranged.

There were only a few weeks left until Christmas and shoppers were streaming in. Kate was kept busy, but not too busy to notice how the land lay. Margo Thompson's narrowed eyes kept darting in Grant's direction and she grew increasingly cool towards Kate as the morning wore on.

Kate smiled to herself. At the earliest opportunity she would put the girl's mind at rest for she had absolutely no interest in Grant Edwards. Margo could feel free, and she hoped the girl had plenty of conversation in store for future dinner parties! Kate's attention was caught by a woman who was peering into a display cabinet.

'May I assist you?' she inquired.

The woman turned.

'Oh, it's you, is it?' Imelda Barnard said scathingly.

'Miss Howard,' the man at her side acknowledged.

'Good morning, Mr Watson. Is there anything I can show you?'

His eyebrows rose.

'You work here?' he asked in surprise.

'Life is full of little surprises, isn't it?' Kate replied.

Miss Barnard's voice was derisive.

'I suppose child-minding occupations are rather poorly paid. This must be very convenient for you, weekend work?'

'Oh, absolutely,' Kate agreed. 'It keeps me in lipstick.'

Grant Edwards hurried over, scenting a quality sale.

'Is there anything you wished to view, madam?' he enquired.

Miss Barnard's eyes glinted, and an arm snaked through Peter Watson's.

'Did you notice that large emerald ring in the window, with hundreds of tiny diamonds, darling? It would be just perfect, don't you think?'

She glanced slyly at Kate, her meaning unmistakable.

'Miss Howard will show you what we

have, madam. As the owner's daughter,' Grant said, trying to impress, 'she will know exactly the sort of thing a woman like yourself requires.'

Then he took himself off importantly, having spotted his next customer.

'Owner?'

Miss Barnard's gaze sharpened on Kate's face.

'This is a family business. I help out occasionally as a favour.'

'The emerald ring?' Miss Barnard prompted.

'No, Imelda,' Peter Watson said firmly. 'We came to see the bracelets. Gold, Miss Howard, if you would be so kind?'

Imelda looked livid but was wise enough to say nothing as Kate extracted a black velvet tray.

'Is this what you had in mind?'

She had underestimated Miss Barnard, however, who appeared determined to view every piece in the shop. Finally even Peter Watson lost patience.

'That one,' he said firmly, pointing to

the one of his choice.

'It's perfect, darling,' Imelda agreed coyly.

'Not at all, Imelda. It is in the form of a thank you. We are all indebted to you. After all it was you who told me where to find Vicky.'

5

Kate eyed the paperwork which had been accumulating on her desk. Hopefully there would be no interruptions this morning.

'Guess what I heard last night?' Pam said as she laid a pile of letters on the desk. 'Remember that glamorous redhead who arrived last week to collect Vicky? She's set to become the new Mrs Watson, I believe.'

'Pam, it's unethical to discuss Mr Watson's affairs unless it's in Vicky's interests.'

'Oh, but it is in her interests. It concerns the child's future stepmother, doesn't it? Miss Barnard is staying with her aunt, and my neighbour knows the aunt. The aunt says that she's a very determined lady. What Imelda wants, Imelda gets, and Imelda wants Peter Watson.'

Pointedly, Kate changed the subject. 'About that school outing this term.'

But Pam was determined to have her say.

'Well, anyway, I'm told that he is quite besotted. Who wouldn't be? She's glamorous, isn't she? An actress, too, I believe, although between you and me the aunt says she's not very good and wants to take up modelling instead. She met Peter Watson just recently in Cape Town and promptly followed him here. Isn't it romantic?'

Kate tried not to show her anger and dismissed Pam with a nod. Some time later, she looked in on the Creative Room, where she noticed Vicky was engrossed in a rather messy cut-and-stick activity. Beside her on the table lay a black crayon drawing which spoke volumes.

'Tell me about your drawing, Vicky,' Kate encouraged. 'Is that you?'

Kate pointed to a small figure at the bottom of the page which was all but obscured by the size of the others. They obviously loomed large in her mind.

'Yes,' Vicky replied.

'And who is this?'

'Felicia.'

'I see.' Not Mummy, Kate noted. 'And the others?'

'Uncle Paul,' Vicky said dully, 'and Uncle André, Felicia's friends. They shout. I don't like them.'

'I don't suppose you do,' Kate agreed gently. 'Still, it's a nice picture.'

'No!' Vicky shrilled. 'It's not! I hate it!'

She snatched up a crayon and began to cover the figures with fierce, angry scribbles. Then she scrunched it into a tight ball and hurled it into the waste bin.

Kate gave her a hug.

'I think we should go into the garden. We might find something unusual out there.'

There were excited cries as they all ran outside with Mrs Reddy. Kate took the opportunity to slip away. She was feeling nervous. Tonight she would present the school's year-end report to the parents at a cheese-and-wine function.

Back home, she had a cool shower, changed into a blue and mauve jersey silk and set off for the evening, feeling slightly more confident, although her knees shook as she rose to address the parents.

'As you all know, Mrs Rattray will be returning in the new year, so this will be my last opportunity to speak to you all.'

His daughter's principal, Peter Watson was thinking, was a most intriguing woman. Contrary to his initial impression, she certainly knew what she was about. Professional to the tips of those elegant sandals, too. Pity that she would soon be leaving the school. She'd done a lot for Vicky.

Kate was continuing but was finding it hard to ignore the presence of Peter Watson. She faltered as her eyes encountered his before going on once again. Afterwards, mingling with people near the buffet table, someone took her arm.

'You're bound to be thirsty after all that.'

Peter Watson placed a glass in her hand.

'I had no idea that infant teaching was so involved,' he added. 'You have given us all a greater understanding from your comments.'

'You and most other people. It's a specialist field.'

Her eyes slid over his tall figure, immaculate in a dark suit, shirt and tie. He seemed terribly sure of himself and it was almost as though he knew what effect he was having on her. She searched for a gap in the crowd.

'I really ought to mingle.'

His eyes gleamed.

'What's the hurry? Besides, I was hoping to speak to you. I've become rather interested in infant education and I've a lot to learn. I imagined Happy Days was nothing more than a glorified crêche.'

Kate took the bait, as he knew she would.

'A common misconception, Mr Watson. Why should you be any different? You've not actually had a child of your own.'

She broke off, embarrassed.

'It's a matter which can be remedied, of course.'

'What is?'

'The lack of children. It involves the increasingly attractive notion of taking a wife. Bachelorhood, Miss Howard, is not always all it's cracked up to be. Having Vicky around of late has shown me what I've been missing. What about you? Do you not want a husband and family?'

'Me?'

'Surely you feel the lack of a man in your life?'

She ignored the question and eyed the faint silver at his temples.

'What about you? At your age the matter must be somewhat pressing. Why not do something? Your Miss Barnard would be thrilled to bits.'

His face told her nothing but she knew she had angered him.

'Oh, but I intend to,' the words came silkily enough, 'and when I find the woman who comes up to my expectations, Miss Howard, I'll let you know. One thing is certain. She will need to be all woman, not part shrew!'

Next day dawned windy and unpleasant, blowing hot and dry. Kate sighed. By the end of the day the children would be unbearably restless and the staff holding on to their tempers. She consulted her watch and decided to go into the garden to monitor the heat. Within the hour the playground would have to be vacated.

It was as though she'd stepped into an oven. The gusty wind tore at her clothing and dust clung to the back of her throat. She spotted the black litter bin rolling over and scattering its contents about the lawn. Then her sandal caught in a gnarled tree root protruding from the dust and she pitched headlong into its choking powder.

Mercifully it was close to the end of the school day. She hobbled inside on a fast-swelling ankle and sat down at her desk.

'I told Vicky to be careful,' a little voice said as Jason peered over the top of it. 'The bees,' he announced dramatically, 'have bitten her.'

'I was careful,' Vicky wailed, as she appeared, 'but I didn't see the bees. It hurts, Miss Howard.'

'Let's have a look.'

Kate sighed. The sting on Vicky's foot was beginning to look ugly and with an effort Kate limped to the cupboard for a tube of ointment. Satisfied, the trio took themselves off. A short while later, Pam suggested that Kate take another look as Vicky's foot had swollen even more.

'Oh, dear, ring Mr Watson please, Pam. He can take his daughter to the doctor immediately. It's almost closing time now, anyway.'

'Mr Watson is not there,' Pam informed her a moment later. 'The housekeeper says he has gone to a cattle sale and Alpheus has already left to collect Vicky from school.'

Kate felt far too hot to deal with any more problems, but she would be forced to handle it herself.

'I'll take her. Might as well ask Dr Mac to look at my ankle, too. Tell Alpheus what's happened and ask him to wait here. I'll have Vicky back at school as soon as possible.'

The doctor, not surprisingly, was running late. After one look at the stream of people ahead of her, Kate asked to use the telephone.

'Please see that Mr Watson's driver is told to return home without Vicky,' she said to one of the kitchen staff who answered the telephone.

It was almost three-thirty when they emerged, hot and tired, from the surgery.

'Vicky, we've both missed our lunch and I'm starving. We'll go to my house first, then I'll take you back to Hazelburn.'

Her father would be none the wiser if she arrived home an hour later.

'I like your house, Miss Howard,' Vicky observed later through a mouthful of sandwich. 'I wish I had an elephant like that.'

She gazed wistfully at the family of wooden elephants marching across the mantelpiece.

'The big one is the daddy,' Vicky decided, 'and the little one's the baby.'

No mention of the mother.

'The baby is called a calf. Would you like to have them?'

She could easily replace the carvings and it seemed such a small price to pay for the child's pleasure. Vicky flung her arms around Kate's neck.

'I wish you were my mummy,' she cried.

To hide her surprise, Kate helped Vicky lift them down and put them carefully into a small cardboard box. By the time she returned from washing the dishes, the little girl was asleep on the sofa. Much in need of a short rest herself, she went to lie down. Hopefully, after half an hour, the pain in her ankle would have lessened and she'd be ready for the drive to Hazelburn.

It was almost dark when Kate opened her eyes and stretched. She switched on the bedside lamp to see the time and decided that supper could wait while she took a shower.

As she reached for the towel, as she came out of the shower, she became aware that her front door was resounding like an African drum. Flinging on her robe, she hurried down the passage to see who was there, uncaring of the pain in her ankle. It was none other than Peter Watson.

'Where is my daughter?' he shouted.

Kate's eyes widened in dismay.

'Vicky! Oh, no! I had forgotten. I'm awfully sorry, Mr Watson!'

'Forgotten what, you incompetent woman?'

His fingers were now digging painfully into the flesh of her arm.

'I returned home less than an hour

ago only to be informed by Alpheus that Vicky had been taken somewhere by some woman for heaven knows what purpose. You'd better come up with some answers, Miss Howard, because I'm holding you responsible. Surely you would have realised that her objectionable mother is not beyond kidnapping her.'

Kate shook his hand off her arm. 'Your daughter is quite safe. There is no need for histrionics! I regret that you have been inconvenienced, but believe it or not, I, too, care about her well-being.'

'On the contrary, it would appear you have been considerably negligent. I want an explanation.'

Ignoring him, Kate turned and limped crossly into the living-room where a sleeping Vicky was sprawled on the sofa, the box of elephants clutched in the crook of her arm. It was evident from the stunned silence that Peter Watson could not quite believe his eyes.

'I am not quite as black as you would

paint me, Mr Watson. Vicky is in no danger. I took her to the doctor to be treated for a bee sting. You could not be reached during the morning because you'd failed to supply your housekeeper with a contact number so I was forced to take her myself for treatment. A message was left for Alpheus but there was obviously a misunderstanding. I then brought Vicky home, gave her some lunch and intended taking her to Hazelburn in time for your return. Unfortunately, after such a trying day, we both fell asleep.'

Kate's ankle was hurting unbearably and she was feeling rather cold.

'I would be obliged if you would take your child now, please, and go.'

To her shame, her voice wobbled. She'd had quite enough of the Watsons for one day, furious with herself for her oversight and even more furious with him for doubting her. What a rude, insufferable bore he was, and quite paranoid about the child's safety. Unaware that her face was an open book, Kate glared at him to keep herself from weeping.

'I'm sorry,' he said quietly, 'you've been most kind.'

'No problem.'

Her voice was as cold as her eyes as she watched Peter Watson bend to lift the sleeping child, reflecting ruefully that anything he tried to say now would only make matters worse. How was he to know she had taken Vicky? And then she'd come to the front door dressed in that robe, with damp tendrils about her neck. Small wonder his blood pressure had shot up.

Next day, Kate tossed a raincoat into the car and drove to school under a bank of low cloud. Her ankle was still tender, the bandage just visible below her black trousers. Thankfully the cooler weather had materialised and the children would be more manageable today.

Vicky arrived with Alpheus, beaming, apparently none the worse for the bee sting. It was unbelievable that this was the same insecure child who had arrived at Happy Days a few weeks ago. Kate went into her office with a small glow of fulfilment.

'The Holly and the Ivy,' she sang while paging through a book of Christmas carols, trying to decide which ones they should have for the Nativity play.

'No, Kate, roses and ivy.'

Pam laid the beautiful basket arrangement on her desk.

'For me? From whom?'

'Some secret admirer?'

Kate took one look at the handwriting on the accompanying envelope. Pam grinned and withdrew. As soon as the door closed, Kate eagerly tore open the envelope.

Allow me to make amends, she read on the card. *Vicky and I will expect you for dinner tonight at Hazelburn. Alpheus will call for you at 7 p.m.*

She threw the card into the bin. If Peter Watson thought she would obey a summons like that in order to ease his conscience, he could think again. There was no way she was spending a whole evening in his presence, and as soon as she got home she would tell him so.

Her phone in the hall was ringing as she opened the door that evening with her arms full of groceries.

'Are you coming to dinner tonight, Miss Howard?' Vicky sounded childishly happy.

Kate swallowed. What's the bet Peter Watson had put her up to this? A pity she would have to be disappointed.

'I'm sorry, Vicky, but I — '

'Won't be manipulated by man nor beast?' Peter Watson intervened smoothly, having taken the receiver from his niece's hand. 'Could we not persuade you otherwise, Miss Howard? Not even if I tell you that Albertina has been slaving over a hot stove all day and Vicky has helped? You wouldn't have the heart to disappoint a small girl, would you?'

'Very well, I'll be there at seven. I shall drive myself. And Mr Watson — '

'Yes?'

'You are utterly shameless.'

'I think that would be a fair assessment.'

He grinned, and rang off.

6

The drizzle which had persisted since late afternoon had finally turned to sheeting rain and visibility was not good when Kate set off. Once the city traffic had been negotiated she turned into the country, eventually arriving at the turn-off to Hazelburn. The car skidded in the mud, which did nothing to improve her temper. Peter Watson really ought to improve his road!

She eventually parked in front of the house and dashed up the veranda steps. The hall smelled of roses and furniture polish. Jewel-coloured oriental carpets covered the gleaming pine floor.

'I'm so glad you've come, Miss Howard,' Vicky said as she hurled herself at Kate. 'The elephants are in bed. The little one was playing up.'

'The little ones usually do,' she agreed, smiling.

Whereupon Vicky decided that the little one probably needed a drink, and promptly went to take care of it.

'May I offer you a drink?' Peter Watson offered.

Kate accepted a glass of sherry and leaned back against the elegant brocaded sofa.

'Mr Watson — '

'It's time we dispensed with the formalities, Kate. The name is Peter.

'Well, all right, but at school I shall still call you Mr Watson.'

'Fair enough.'

'You needn't have sent those flowers,' she blurted out. 'It wasn't necessary, but thank you.'

Kate watched as he poured another drink. It was crazy to feel this way but she couldn't take her eyes off him. When he was in the room it was as though no-one else existed.

'Do you mind if we dine early so that Albertina can put Vicky to bed?'

'Not at all,' she replied, and for the second time in as many minutes Kate was floored. Peter Watson was turning into quite a good father, after all.

Albertina had worked wonders over the meal, and Peter carved the lamb expertly, proving to be a competent host. Albertina brought the coffee tray into the living-room and took Vicky away to bed.

'Do you realise,' Kate asked slowly, 'how much Vicky has blossomed since she's been here?'

'Indeed I do. It makes it all the more difficult to forgive myself. I should have wised up sooner.'

'But you had no way of knowing she was being so mistreated.'

'I should have made it my business. I allowed myself to become too wrapped up in my work. When Tom, my brother, was dying, he asked me to take care of Vicky, adopt her if necessary. He sounded quite desperate, and I thought it was merely the ramblings of a very ill man. He obviously knew his wife. I thought the child needed her mother. How wrong can one be?'

'You're not to be too hard on yourself. Besides, you're making it up to Vicky now.'

'Thank you, Kate.'

The evening over, he was helping her into her coat when she'd surprised a look in his eyes, quickly veiled.

'Thank you for a lovely evening,' she began, but her words were cut off by his light kiss, a simple gesture of friendship.

Then she'd blown it. Powerful feelings she thought she'd buried rose up and she'd kissed him back, her arms creeping around his neck. His kiss had changed then, and he'd drawn her hard against his body.

'Well, well.' There was a gleam in the sapphire eyes. 'In my day, schoolma'ams didn't behave like this.'

Kate scrambled out to her car in heavy rain and fumbled in the dark for the ignition. Switching it on, she lurched down the track, resisting the urge to look in her rear-view mirror. Her face was suffused with colour. Whatever must he think? She'd thrown herself at him like a love-sick schoolgirl!

Her hands gripped the steering-wheel as she thought about that kiss. How could she? For a school principal to throw herself at one of the parents like that was unprofessional beyond belief! The car headlights failed to pierce the thick African night and in the end Kate was forced to drive by instinct rather than sight. Unfortunately, instinct failed.

The road which had been awash on her arrival was now a muddy torrent. The car veered uncontrollably to one side and skidded into a deep rut. Finding herself suspended at an impossible angle, Kate tried to control her feeling of alarm. This was all Peter Watson's fault! If he kept his roads in better repair this would never have happened!

The rain pelted on the roof. She had two choices — sit there suspended all night, damp and miserable, or she could climb out, squelch up to the house and beg a bed for the night. It was against her better judgment to choose the latter.

Anyway, the door of the car appeared to be wedged fast against the bank. Tomorrow was Saturday and she didn't have to be at school. She closed her eyes, preparing to spend a most uncomfortable night. Every muscle in her back seemed to be aching and the seat-belt was interfering with her breathing. Eventually she unlatched it, tumbled over towards the passenger door and opened it against the force of the wind.

Hoisting herself up the bank by holding on to protruding roots, she managed to reach the track. With a little sob Kate thrust the wet hair from her face and began the long trek back up the hall. By the time the lights of Hazelburn came into view, her ankle was causing considerable discomfort. Her face, rain-stung and flushed from the exertion of scurrying up the hill, was a sight. Peter stared incredulously at the apparition on his doorstep.

'Good grief! And to think I once found you attractive!'

His mockery was the last straw.

'I could have drowned!' she spat, beginning to shake with reaction.

A large pool of water was collecting on the expensive carpet, but she was beyond caring.

'I've just driven into a rut, and its all your wretched fault. Your road is appalling! I had to climb out of an almost overturned car and run all the way back in the dark and all you can do is stand there and laugh!'

'Kate!'

He reached for her but she pushed past and fled down the passage to the bathroom where she burst into tears. A hot shower did much to restore her. She rubbed her hair almost dry and put on the huge towelling robe which was hanging behind the door. Collecting her sodden clothing into a sorry-looking pile she went to the kitchen in search of a plastic bag.

'Give me those. Albertina will see to

them in the morning. Drink this.'

He thrust a steaming mug into her hands.

'You'll stay overnight and I'll see to the car in the morning.'

'I would have made it if your track had been better maintained.'

'I agree it's a disgrace.'

His eyes were on her face. If only she knew how he longed to take her in his arms. Instead he leaned forward and gave her a brief, hard kiss. Kate stepped back quickly. She wasn't about to make a fool of herself twice in one night. Fiercely she pulled the robe about her.

'Good-night!'

She was halfway down the passage when a thought occurred to her. Sheepishly she returned to the kitchen.

'Where do I sleep?'

'If you hadn't been in such a hurry to escape, I'd have shown you. The guest room is next to Vicky's and it's already prepared because I'm expecting a guest tomorrow. Good-night, Kate.'

The room near Vicky's, she thought

exhaustedly, and hurried inside. The duvet on the king-sized bed looked marvellous. She slipped out of the robe, flung herself under its warmth and was asleep within minutes.

Daylight was streaming in through blue curtains and wonderful birdsong sounded from the trees beyond. The weavers weren't usually this vociferous, Kate thought, and opened her eyes. Those were not her birds and this was not her bedroom! She sat upright and noticed what she'd failed to see the previous evening. The room was not a guest room.

Kate threw off the covers and rushed into the ensuite bathroom only to find it was full of masculine toiletries. Her cheeks pink, she put on the robe and went in search of her clothes. Albertina was vacuuming the passage and stared curiously as Kate emerged from the bedroom.

'I bring your clothes now?' she enquired politely, and a few minutes later Kate was scrambling into clothes still warm from the drier.

She used a comb she found in the bathroom to tidy her hair and ventured into the dining-room.

'Sleep well?' Peter Watson enquired blandly.

'I'm awfully sorry. I slept in your bed, didn't I? Where did you sleep?'

'I was comfortable enough.'

Vicky entered the dining-room, clutching a doll.

'Uncle Peter, Georgina wants some egg and ba — '

She stared.

'Has Miss Howard come for break-fast, too?'

'Miss Howard hasn't been home yet. She stayed overnight.'

'Oh. Which room did you sleep in, Miss Howard?'

'Mine,' her uncle said outrageously.

Kate glared at Peter. Didn't he know that such irresponsible talk in front of a child could be innocently repeated? He disappeared after breakfast with the explanation that he needed to instruct his workers. Albertina, he said, would bring her tea at eleven, on the veranda. By two-thirty, Kate was becoming exasperated. She and Vicky had had both tea and lunch and were on the veranda again when he came striding over the lawn.

Albertina had outdone herself with more cream scones and fruit cake. Kate began to pour from the large silver teapot.

The peace was suddenly shattered by the roar of a yellow sport car on the drive. It stopped with a squeal and a pair of long legs thrust themselves from the driving seat, followed by the well-clad body of Miss Barnard. She picked her way over the lawn and exclaimed in annoyance at the way the tall heels of her sandals sank into its soggy depths. Peter schooled his face and rose to greet her.

'I wasn't expecting you until later, Imelda.'

'I know, darling, but I simply couldn't wait.'

Her mouth dropped open at the sight of Kate presiding over the teapot. Her eyes darted speculatively from one to the other.

'A cup of tea?' Peter invited smoothly.

'Black, no sugar,' she informed Kate, adding with a coy glance at Peter. 'I have to watch my figure, although one day soon I hope to give up acting and modelling to become a lady of leisure.'

Peter watched the tightening of Kate's lips. Vicky offered Imelda the plate of scones. She waved the child away. Unimpressed, Vicky stuffed her mouth with another scone. Kate busied herself with the teapot and tried not to catch Peter's eye.

'Vicky,' she intervened gently after the third scone had disappeared, 'I think you've had enough, don't you? You won't want to spoil your dinner.'

Imelda's eyes flashed.

'You aren't in the schoolroom now, Miss Howard! Leave the child alone.'

There was a moment's silence into

which Vicky's unaccountable observation was dropped.

'Miss Howard,' she piped up, 'slept in Uncle Peter's bed last night.'

Peter sighed softly, amusement well concealed behind a bland mask. Kate drained her cup and stood up.

'Hadn't we better see to my car?' she asked tightly.

Peter stood up and pulled Kate's car keys from his pocket.

'Your car has already been seen to, Kate. You'll find it clean and waiting in the garage next to mine.'

She thanked him politely and left.

7

Kate poured cream over the raspberry mousse while her mother eyed her in concern.

'You're looking strained, Kate. You ought to relax and socialise a bit more, dear. You're working too hard.'

'You'll be pleased to know I've contacted Sarah.'

'You have? That's nice. She married that Doug fellow, didn't she?'

'Doug Gray. I'm seeing them tomorrow evening, in fact. Been invited to a swimming party at their place, with a barbecue afterwards.'

Mrs Howard watched her daughter covertly.

'By the way, I saw Elizabeh Watson. She's your Peter Watson's mother. She says that her grandchild just adores you. I believe you gave her a set of carved elephants.'

'How news travels! Yes, I did. Shall I do the dishes?'

'Just stack them for later. Let's have our coffee in the sitting-room. By the way, Peter Watson seems such a nice man. He told me all about Vicky and how good you have been for her.'

'Since when have you been on speaking terms with him? Mother! Where did you meet him, then?' Kate demanded.

Mrs Howard hid a smile.

'At church.'

It would appear there were one or two things she didn't know about Mr Watson, Kate thought, as she headed back to her apartment.

By late afternoon the following day, the sun was blazing and Kate couldn't wait for that swim at Sarah's. It would be such fun to take up where she and her friends had left off. After feeding Sebastian, she locked the flat and drove across town to her friend's home.

'Wow!' Sarah greeted her. 'You look stunning!'

'You're not bad yourself.' Kate hugged her friend.

'Come on in. My goodness, it's nice to see you again.'

Doug appeared and thrust a tall glass into her hand, inviting her to join the others at the poolside. Kate thanked him and wandered into the garden.

'Let me introduce you to some of the others,' Doug offered.

The first person she saw was Grant Edwards. He eyed her approvingly before placing a proprietary arm about her shoulders. If Kate's greeting was less than warm he seemed not to notice.

'You know Margo from work, of course?' he was saying.

'Of course.'

She smiled but Margo only nodded and warily sized up the opposition. Under cover of the conversation Kate resolved to put her out of her misery.

'Relax, Margo, he's all yours,' she whispered.

'There's someone I'd like you to

meet,' Sarah said as Kate emerged later in her swimsuit. 'He's an absolute dish, and if I weren't a happily married woman I'd be making a play myself. Meet the most eligible bachelor in the area, Peter Watson. Peter, this is an old school friend of mine, Kate Howard.'

Peter Watson's eyes flicked over Kate's tanned legs.

'We've met,' he clipped, a faintly sardonic gleam in his eyes.

Kate felt her breath catch in her throat. He looked magnificent in the black swimming trunks which hugged his lean hips, his bronzed body glistening with pool water. She tore her eyes away and quickly drew her towel around her, inventing a hasty excuse to make for the pool.

The water cooled her heated skin as she swam to the opposite side of the pool hoping to put as much distance between herself and Peter as she could. Reaching the other side Kate placed her palms carefully on the tiled surround and made to pull herself out. Strong, warm hands grabbed her waist from behind and drew her inelegantly back into the water.

'Allow me to help you out,' he said smoothly.

'I can manage,' she stated angrily.

'Kate . . . '

He gripped her by the waist and drew her suddenly against him so that she was forced to look into his face, afraid that the trembling of her body would betray her.

'Yes?'

He stared into her eyes for a long moment before brushing her lips with his own in a little feather of promise.

'Keep your hands off me, Peter Watson!' she choked out. 'I'm not interested. How many times must I say it?'

He released her immediately.

'Message received,' he drawled, 'loud and clear.'

The water rippled as a woman squeezed herself between them.

'Imelda,' Peter greeted her. 'I thought

you said you couldn't make it.'

'I changed my mind, and a good thing, too. So good of you, Miss Howard, to keep Peter entertained but we won't detain you any longer.'

Kate, only too pleased to make herself scarce, climbed out of the pool. She went into the house once more to change, unaware of the look in Peter's eyes as they followed her, or of the malice in his companion's as she observed him. Not long now, Imelda thought, and her brother would be arriving from Cape Town, as she'd planned. With both Vicky and Kate out of the way, Peter Watson would be hers, and hers alone.

The evening sun highlighted Kate's brown hair and skin so that it shone like clear honey as they sat around the barbecue. Peter sat nearby.

'It's a good thing I'm a happily married man, Kate,' Doug joked, handing her a glass of wine. 'If it's any consolation, Sarah and I were just saying that your ex-fiancé needs his head examined. Don't you think so, Peter?'

Peter was saved from immediate reply by the arrival of Imelda from the kitchen with some meat for the barbecue. He took the meat from her without a word and became ostensibly engrossed in placing it on the grid.

'Miss Howard's love life,' he informed a startled Doug, 'holds no interest for me whatsoever.'

With which sentiment Miss Barnard appeared heartily to concur. She pressed herself against Peter and slanted Kate a malicious glance.

Vicky was absent from school on the Monday. Kate examined the registers and enquired idly whether Mr Watson had telephoned about Vicky.

'No,' Pam said, 'but I'll let you know if he does.'

On Tuesday she was still absent but when she arrived on Wednesday morning it was with happy tales of her stay with Granny Elizabeth.

'Uncle Peter,' she explained, 'went

swimming so I went to Granny Elizabeth's house and then I just stayed and stayed.'

'I see!'

Peter Watson had selfishly made the party into an extended weekend with Imelda! Kate knew she was prying.

'Where does your grandmother live?'

'Near the racecourse.'

'You mean the one in Pietermaritzburg?'

That was only forty minutes' drive away. He could easily have had Vicky back in time for school on Monday.

When she failed to turn up again on Thursday, however, Kate became uneasy. What was Peter Watson playing at? Didn't he realise that Vicky, of all children, needed routine and stability? It was one thing palming her off on his mother for the weekend but quite another when it came to hitting the high spots during the week as well.

By Friday morning, Kate was hopping mad, without quite stopping to analyse why. It was a particularly hot, trying day and her head was beginning to throb as she picked up the telephone.

'Hello?' Albertina answered, and went to summon her employer.

'Mr Watson,' Kate demanded, 'what has happened to Vicky?'

'Ah, good morning to you, too, Kate.'

'Oh, er, good morning.'

'I take it from your tone that it isn't a good one at all.'

'Mr Watson,' she waded in, 'I feel bound to point out that your treatment of Vicky leaves a lot to be desired.'

'I beg your pardon?'

'Your daughter is hardly being allowed to, quote, develop in a normal and healthy way, unquote.'

'What is it that you are trying to say, precisely?'

'Well, it's the matter of your private life.'

Kate hesitated. This might not be as easy as she'd imagined, but it had to be said, in Vicky's interests, of course.

'Forgive the lack of intelligence, Miss Howard, but I fail to see what the problem is. I'm afraid you'll have to spell it out.'

'When it comes to Vicky's attendance or lack of it, it becomes the school's affair. As her principal, I have a right to query it.'

'So that's what's bugging you. Would you be so kind,' he drawled, 'as to tell me what it is I'm supposed to have done with my private life? I am sure you'd be only too pleased to enlighten me.'

'If you choose to carouse all weekend with a certain lady, so be it, it's nothing to do with me. But for pity's sake, try, for Vicky's education, to at least restrain yourself during the week, Mr Watson!'

There was a strangled sound at the other end of the line.

'Miss Howard,' he managed, 'would you do something for me?'

'Certainly, Mr Watson.'

'Find yourself a man.'

For a full minute after he had hung up, Kate was still blinking in outrage. The phone tinkled and she picked it up automatically, thinking it was Pam.

'Yes?'

By now, Peter Watson had himself well in hand.

'I would like to apologise for that last remark.'

He sounded suspiciously humble.

'It was uncalled for. It remains patently obvious, Miss Howard, that I have certain failings as parent material. I'm convinced I could benefit from some of your expert advice. Could you possibly see your way clear to calling round here after school today? I know it's a lot to ask but, well, it is in the interests of Vicky's education, and I think there are a few things we need to clarify.'

'Expect me at two-thirty, Mr Watson.'

She dashed home to feed Sebastian and freshen up, pushing aside any lingering doubts about the rash promise she'd made. She was doing this for Vicky, and no-one else. Another thing, Vicky would soon be having a birthday, according to the records. What kind of occasion would it be without a guardian who toed the line? It was bad enough with an absentee mother!

Everything was quiet as Kate walked up the veranda steps at Hazelburn, much too quiet. When her third knock went unanswered, she stepped purposefully into the silent hall, her steps masked by the carpets. In the living-room not a soul was in sight. She flung her handbag on to the sofa and went down the passage.

Where was everyone? Peter Watson had been told exactly when to expect her, so where was he? At Vicky's door she stopped short. Peter appeared to be asleep in a large armchair next to the bed, his long legs stretched out before him. Lines of fatigue etched his eyes. Vicky, too, was asleep. She was the colour of tomatoes and stirred feverishly.

'Water,' she murmured.

Kate sprang into action, handing her the glass beside the bed. Vicky gulped greedily and fell back, asleep again within seconds. Why hadn't he said the child had measles? She stood transfixed, trying to remember what she'd said on the telephone. He must have been laughing up his sleeve! She turned to slip away.

'Oh, no you don't,' a voice mocked as a hand snaked out and caught the silky material of her skirt, jerking her to a halt.

Sleep-dazed eyes fastened on her inscrutably.

'You can't walk out on me now. You have that all-important advice to dispense, remember?'

'Let me go!' she protested and tried to escape his hold.

'Proceed, Miss Howard. I'm all ears.'

He jerked her skirt again and Kate landed on his lap. His arms tightened about her.

'Carry on. I have all day in which to listen.'

'I . . . '

'Was mistaken? You most certainly were.'

'Look, I apologise, all right? Now let me go.'

'Such humility, Kate! Where's all that wrath and indignation? Don't tell me the shrew has been tamed!'

'I admit I judged you a little hastily,' Kate began woodenly, 'but you must admit that I had Vicky's interests at heart.'

He let her go abruptly and stood up, making her unaccountably nervous.

'You appear to have everything admirably under control, Mr Watson, so I will leave you in peace. My hand-bag — '

She bolted to the living-room.

'Albertina will be mortally offended if you don't sample her teacakes,' he wheedled. 'We'll take it on the veranda,' he said firmly, taking her by the arm. 'Much cooler there.'

There were no teacakes, however, but a packet of biscuits, hastily opened by the housekeeper. Kate smiled reluctantly.

'You've had the doctor out, I suppose?'

'This morning. Never been so pleased

to see him in my life. I'd no idea that sitting up all night with a sick child was so terrifying.'

'Vicky should be fine as long as you follow all the advice you've been given. German measles is a common enough illness.'

He was observing her with a pathetic kind of desperation.

'I have no right to ask it, of course, but . . . '

'But what?'

'Would you consider staying here overnight to give me a hand, Kate?'

Kate's compassionate nature again responded, against her better judgment.

'Well, only for Vicky's sake, to ensure that you do what the doctor said.'

'Quite so.' His eyes gleamed. 'I'm indebted to you, Kate. And don't worry about night clothes. There's a whole wardrobe of them in the guest room.'

At the look on Kate's face, he grinned.

'Belonging to my sister, Gillian, of course. See you at dinner.'

He strode off to the milking sheds, whistling.

Kate returned the tea tray to the kitchen where Albertina was preparing the evening meal. She smiled delightedly on hearing that Miss Howard was to take charge of Vicky for the night and hastened to make her point.

'She is needing a mother, that little one.'

Kate nodded in agreement. Albertina shouldn't have too long to wait before Imelda was installed. Albertina had a further observation to make.

'Boss must not marry the one with the red hair. Vicky does not like her.'

'No?'

'No. Vicky,' the housekeeper confided, 'likes you!'

Vicky was unable to eat her supper, feeling miserable. She began to cry.

'Never mind, love. You'll feel better in a little while,' Kate soothed.

'Where's Uncle Peter?'

'Here.'

He had been watching from the doorway.

'I'll read you a story while Miss Howard takes away the tray. What would we do without her?'

'You'd manage fine, and well you know it,' Kate snapped.

'A drink before dinner, Kate?' he enquired once Vicky was settled.

'Thank you.'

She accepted a glass and sank into the living-room sofa.

'Now, while we're about it, shall we put aside all past misunderstandings, prejudice and ill-humour? So bad for the digestion.'

Kate gave a reluctant smile. It would do no harm, surely, to drop her defences for one evening, especially as he was in such an endearing mood. She settled back and missed the flash of satisfaction in his blue eyes.

Albertina had taken the trouble to lay out the best silver. Spotless crystal winked in the light of a flickering candelabra on the oak sideboard and there was a dainty centrepiece of sweetpeas. If Kate hadn't known better, she'd have thought this the perfect setting for the big seduction.

Peter guessed her thoughts exactly.

'We shall have to disappoint Albertina,' he said, 'because you and I both know that she is wasting her time trying to bring us together, isn't she?'

8

Kate poured coffee while Peter switched on a rosy lamp and then drew pink velvet curtains. It had dawned on her during the past hour that he was not quite the country bumpkin she would have liked to imagine. Beneath all that laid-back geniality lay a razor-sharp mind and she would do well to remember it.

It seemed imperative suddenly to dispel the intimacy of sharing an evening with him.

'May we take a walk?'

'By all means. I usually take the dogs out at this time, anyway.'

'But what about Vicky?'

'Albertina always waits until I return. We won't be long.'

He whistled for the dogs as Kate went to fetch a cardigan. The sky was bright with stars and it was easy to see the track leading through the trees. Beyond it, stretching silver under a full moon, lay a patch of veld where Amy and Sheena darted to investigate every scent which took their fancy.

'The night scents seem sharper when one is not distracted by the bright light of day, don't they?' Kate said.

'That's one of the things which is so special about an African night,' Peter agreed softly, more interested in the way the moon lit Kate's profile.

The dogs raced ahead, well used to the terrain, but Kate was having a little difficulty with the ruts and boulders. Peter took her arm, looking ruefully at her dainty footwear.

'It will be easier once we reach the other track.'

'Can you smell those scented creepers?' she gabbled on. 'I read somewhere that the flowers actually increase their scent at night to attract the hawk moths. Of course, the scent evaporates during the heat of the day.'

'You're a mine of information, Kate.'

He stopped, reaching for a strand of her hair and twisting it around his finger in the moonlight. For a second his eyes burned into hers before his mouth descended in a brief, exploratory kiss before he gathered her into his arms, intent on prolonging the experience.

All at once he stiffened, thrusting her aside, his eyes intent as he scanned the pines where an owl hooted eerily. He stood listening intently. The moon had disappeared behind scudding clouds.

'What is it?' Kate whispered.

'We have a visitor.'

'At this time of night?'

As they listened, a sports car droned over the hill, changed gear, slowed down and then stopped altogether leaving only the sounds of the African night.

'Do you think — '

'Sshh,' Peter cautioned, gripping her arm, his expression thoughtful. 'We'll go back, now,' he said, helping her once more over the rough terrain and carrying on a rambling conversation about nothing in particular.

As they approached the house he paused, scanned the horizon and listened once more.

'Kate,' he said casually, 'I want you to go inside with the dogs and lock all the doors. I won't be long.'

He gave her a little push, waited until she was safely inside and disappeared in the direction of the pines.

After Albertina had left, she went through the silent house ensuring that the windows were secure and the doors locked. Eventually she decided to have a bath. Then she found a nightdress and matching robe in the guest room, just as he'd said. After checking that Vicky was asleep, she climbed into bed. Kate was almost asleep herself when a light tap sounded on her window pane. Alarmed, she padded to the window.

It was Peter, motioning for her to unlock the kitchen door.

'What kept you?' she demanded as she let him in, eyeing his grim face and dishevelled appearance.

He was still breathing hard and there was a small graze on one cheek.

'One thing and another. Is Vicky asleep?'

'Yes, I've just checked.'

He strode past to see for himself. Reassured, he then returned to the kitchen.

'I could do with a drink. Coffee?'

She nodded.

'Is anything wrong?'

He did not answer immediately but continued to survey the lawn. Then seemingly satisfied, he yanked the curtains closed, flicked on the light switch and calmly reached for two mugs.

'Will you tell me what's going on?' she asked.

'Why should anything be going on?'

'I'm not a fool, you know. That car which arrived earlier, has it gone?'

'It's gone.'

'It was Miss Barnard's car, wasn't it?'

His eyes narrowed.

'How did you know that?'

'Come off it, anyone knows the sound of her car. If you want her to visit you and I'm in the way, just say so? There was no need to meet her in the wood.'

'I do not want Imelda's company, is that quite clear? For your information, that was her car, but she was not in it.'

'Who was, then?'

'Some fool from Cape Town who calls himself Paul. Apparently he didn't quite realise he was trespassing.'

'Well, it has nothing to do with me,' Kate pointed out.

'You're right, it hasn't, but seeing you're so interested, you're going to hear the whole sorry story. It's called feminine curiosity, and you're dying to know why I caught him sneaking through the pines.'

Kate gave a reluctant smile.

'So?'

His eyes held an answering gleam.

'Paul Barnard arrived in town last night, according to my sources, so I can't say I haven't been expecting him. He's an ex-boyfriend of Felicia's with the mistaken idea that if he could return Vicky, she would be so grateful she'd take him back. Like I said,' he finished in disgust, 'he's a complete fool!'

He smiled mirthlessly.

'He nearly had a heart attack when he discovered I was trailing him. He was snooping around Vicky's bedroom window, obviously having been well primed as to its whereabouts.'

Kate was shocked.

'How awful! What did you do?'

'Let's just say I disabused him of any notion that I'd part with my niece. I doubt he'll be back.'

He smiled grimly, and picked up the tray.

'We'll have our cocoa in the living-room. And then it's bed.'

Kate slept late next morning. She stumbled into the bathroom where the mirror revealed a tired face beneath tousled hair.

Vicky, pale but in good spirits, insisted on being allowed up to play.

'It won't do you any harm,' Kate told her, 'providing you keep warm and lie down again when you're tired.'

'Surely a little fresh air won't come amiss?' Peter suggested. 'It's such a lovely morning. I thought we'd take a short ride to the dam. There's a pair of nesting coots I'd like to show you both.'

Kate shrugged.

'Whatever, but I ought to be going home, now that Vicky is feeling a little better.'

Vicky threw herself at Kate, suddenly insecure.

'Don't go, Miss Howard, please don't go.'

'Well, I suppose I could stay for another hour or two, but after that I must go home, because of Sebastian. He'll be wondering where his dinner is. Of course, you'll be busy yourself, what with having to feed those elephants, remember?'

Vicky brightened.

'Let's pretend we're elephants. You,' she told her uncle, 'are the daddy, Miss Howard is the mummy, and I'll be the baby.'

Kate entered lightly into the game as the Land Rover bounced towards the dam. Vicky obviously needed to play out her fantasy.

'We'll all live at the dam for ever and ever,' she continued, indicating her need for some sort of family stability.

Kate hid her anger as she stepped from the vehicle. If Peter wished to make his small niece feel more secure, he'd better make up his mind which female he wanted, and then marry her! A commotion in the shallow water distracted them as two red-knobbed coots held a stand-up fight, rising literally from the water chest to chest and flailing with wings and feet.

'Which one is the mother?' Vicky wanted to know.

'Sshh,' her uncle cautioned. 'Follow me and I'll show you.'

At their approach, a brooding female

flapped from her nest in the reeds and disappeared beneath the water. Peter hefted Vicky on to his shoulder to gain a better view of the semi-floating nest with its clutch of eggs.

'Will the mother come back to the nest?' Vicky asked.

The underlying anxiety in the question was not lost on adults.

'Of course she will,' Kate reassured her.

'Does she love her babies?' Vicky persisted.

'Yes, mothers love their babies and try to take care of them,' Kate replied.

Vicky accepted this doubtfully and skipped away.

'I must take issue with you, Kate. Not all mothers love their young, human ones, that is,' Peter said grimly. 'Vicky's mother being a case in point. Felicia spent her days flitting around the country performing, and totally oblivious of her responsibilities. She has an adoring public, all right, mostly male! My brother left her well off, but she went through everything in no time, including Vicky's inheritance. She only married Mark for his money in the first place. I begged him to leave her alone, but he wouldn't listen, said he loved her. What could I do?'

'Does Vicky ever speak of her mother?'

'Seldom. No love lost there, it seems. No real bonding. How can you relate to a mother who treats you as though you don't exist? I find it extremely difficult to forgive Felicia for what she did to her little daughter.'

The drive back was somewhat silent, with Vicky asleep on the back seat. On their return, they saw a familiar sports car in the drive and Kate's heart sank.

'Peter, darling,' Imelda scolded, immaculate as ever. 'Where have you been? I've been waiting ages! I thought I'd just arrive and surprise you.'

She caught sight of Kate emerging from the vehicle and her jaw dropped.

'Well! I see we have a visitor.'

Peter greeted Imelda smoothly and

lifted a sleeping Vicky from the vehicle.

'Would you ladies kindly take yourselves inside while I put Vicky to bed? Oh, and ask Albertina to make some tea, will you?'

He disappeared into the house. Immediately Imelda took charge.

'No need for you to concern yourself, Miss Howard,' she effected the gracious hostess. 'Do go into the sitting-room while I see to things.'

'As you like.'

Kate went instead to her bedroom to tidy herself and when she reappeared, Imelda had kicked off her gold high-heeled sandals and was reclining on the sofa. She lost no time in ascertaining if Kate had once more spent the night at Hazelburn.

'It is hardly any of your business, Imelda, but, yes, I did.'

'I must warn you that Peter is simply not interested in the likes of you. You don't have much style, do you? I mean, that skirt looks as though it's been through a bush backwards.'

'Who's been through a bush backwards?' Peter asked with a hint of amusement as he entered the room.

'I was just giving Miss Howard a few tips on how to dress, you know. Being a model, I know one or two things, and I like to be generous with my advice.'

'I see. Pour the tea will you, Kate?'

Imelda's triumph disappeared. She opened her mouth to say something and closed it again, deciding to accept the cup Kate was offering, with as much grace as she could muster. She turned to Peter.

'What on earth did you say to that brother of mine last night, darling? He came home from Hazelburn looking rather white, and this morning he just packed his bags and left. I do think it was the teeniest bit unkind of you. After all, he took a special trip up here at his own expense.'

'Nobody asked him to come.'

'Perhaps not, but he just wanted to check up on Vicky so he could reassure

Felicia she was being properly cared for.'

Peter concealed his feelings beneath a bland mask but his eyes were cold.

'Is that so?'

'And how is the poor little poppet today?' Imelda queried sweetly.

'Vicky? I'm afraid she has German measles. Kate very kindly stayed overnight to keep an eye on her.'

'How good of Miss Howard. I'm afraid I'm hopeless with the sick. But do call on me for other things, darling.'

'Thank you, Imelda, but everything's under control now. You'll stay to lunch?'

'Of course, and then perhaps I could give Miss Howard a lift back to Bothatown.'

She slanted Kate a sly glance. Kate was equally determined she would not be spending another night under Peter's roof.

'I have my own car, thank you. I'll be leaving shortly.'

'Oh, good.'

Imelda's satisfaction was barely concealed.

'When do you plan to return to Cape Town, Imelda?' Kate inquired.

'Who said I was returning? I've no immediate plans, Miss Howard. It all rather depends.'

She gave Peter the full benefit of her theatrical smile.

'On what?' Kate persisted.

'Oh, on other considerations.'

Rudely she turned away.

9

There were just three weeks to go before Happy Days closed for the long summer holiday. It crossed Kate's mind that she should start looking for another job, but she was just too busy. After the Nativity play would come stocktaking and a mountain of paper-work which had to be dealt with. She had made a start but at this rate she'd be working late after school each day.

The weekend stretched before Kate like an empty exercise book. She climbed into her car, wondering how to fill in the hours, and on impulse took the road which led to her parents' home. After a cup of tea with her mother she'd stop at a nearby shopping mall for a video or two.

Mrs Howard was in the garden picking dead heads from a clump of daisy bushes.

'What a lovely surprise, darling. I was about to go in for tea, and there's some cherry cake left over. Had a good day?'

'So-so.'

'Put the kettle on, while I wash my hands.'

After a pleasant day, Kate headed home. The telephone was ringing as she unlocked her front door. She snatched up the receiver.

'At last!' Peter Watson complained. 'Where have you been?'

'Out.' Kate's voice was frosty. 'What do you want?'

'A favour.'

'Like what?' she asked cautiously.

'Would you help me out, Kate? I wouldn't do this if it weren't such an emergency. Would you be so kind as to allow Vicky to stay overnight? I know it's rather an imposition and you must feel free to refuse, but quite frankly, there is nobody else I can trust. There's no time to take her to my mother in Pietermaritzburg and I need to be with my sister, Gillian, as soon as possible.

My brother-in-law, a game ranger, has been seriously injured by a white rhino.'

'All right,' Kate said resignedly. 'I'd be glad to help.'

There was just enough time to feed Sebastian and make up a bed in the spare room before they arrived.

'I can't say exactly when I will call for her tomorrow. It rather depends on Tim's condition. Gillian and I will stay with my mother tonight and then I'll return some time during tomorrow afternoon. Would that do?'

'Perfectly. And don't worry about Vicky, I'll take good care of her.'

'I know.'

He dropped a surprise quick kiss on her lips and was gone.

'May I give Sebastian some milk?' Vicky asked before bedtime.

Kate opened the refrigerator.

'Oh, dear, we've run out. We'll be needing some for our cereal in the morning so we'd better take a walk to the corner shop.'

In the shop, Vicky skipped happily

past the chocolates and magazines and then cannoned rather clumsily into the postcards.

'Stupid child,' a woman nearby muttered. 'Oh! It's you, Vicky.' She looked around expectantly. 'Where's your father?'

Vicky picked herself up off the floor.

'He's not here. I'm staying with Miss Howard.'

'Miss Howard?' Imelda's eyes glittered. 'What on earth for?'

Kate came up with a polite greeting and suggested she and Vicky move on to the freezer section.

'Just a moment, Miss Howard. Where's Peter? What are you doing with the child?'

'I won't satisfy your more than avid curiosity, Imelda. Goodbye!'

At the house, Kate bent to unlatch the front gate, unaware of the yellow sports car which had been cruising at a discreet distance behind them. The owner's eyes held frustration as they searched the street fruitlessly for a grey

BMW. Relieved, Imelda drew to a smooth halt beyond the gate. Obviously Vicky's father wasn't about to spend the evening with Miss Howard, which was one consolation! What was it about the man? She, like Felicia, was used to men falling at her feet. With Peter, she was the one who was doing all the running. It made him all the more desirable, of course.

Imelda slid the car into gear. All that money, too! She grimaced regretfully as she thought of her brother's failed ploy the previous evening to gain access to Hazelburn. If only he'd been able to seize Vicky, Peter Watson would have paid handsomely to get the child back, or so Felicia had said.

Of course, Peter need never know that Imelda herself had been involved. She would just have collected her part of the payout and sat tight. Still, she was a resourceful person. She would think of something. Imelda Barnard might have grown up poor but she had no intention of remaining so. She intended to marry money and no-one would stop her, least of all that snooty schoolma'am.

With a vicious jab at the accelerator she roared off.

Kate and Vicky woke next morning to a beautiful day, and Kate hurried through her chores while Vicky sat with a puzzle. They would take a picnic lunch to the park and feed the ducks.

'May I take Sebastian into the garden?'

'Of course, Vicky.'

Kate unlocked the door and went to secure the front gate which opened directly on to the pavement.

'On no account go outside into the street, Vicky. Is that clear?'

'Yes. Don't forget the bread for the ducks, Miss Howard.'

'I won't.'

Kate returned to the kitchen to boil some eggs for sandwiches. Ten minutes later she placed the hamper on the doorstep and called for Vicky to use the bathroom before they left. There was no reply.

'Vicky!' she called again. 'Hurry up, love.'

Sebastian was sitting on the wall in the sunshine. Kate went down the front steps into the garden.

'Vicky! Where are you hiding?' She peeped around the azalea bushes. 'It's time to go!'

The garden was empty, and with a sigh, she retraced her steps thinking that Vicky had already slipped past her into the house. But a thorough search proved otherwise, and Kate's heart began to pound. She ran once more into the garden and called, but no small figure in red T-shirt and jeans emerged. Kate's disquiet turned to panic.

She scanned the garden again and saw something which chilled her blood. The gate was ajar. Frantically rushing out on to the pavement Kate scanned the street. Still no Vicky.

She had left the front door open but ran, uncaring, to the shop on the corner. Perhaps the child had wanted another ice-cream. Yes, that was it! She'd gone to the shop. Before Kate reached it, however, she knew the effort was in vain.

Enquiries elicited nothing and despair clutched her heart in an icy vice. She raced home and reached for the telephone with trembling fingers. Dear God, please take care of her.

The front gate clicked and Kate crashed the receiver on to its cradle. Thank God! That would be Vicky. She raced to the door. Peter Watson was slinging his jacket wearily over one shoulder. He looked up and saw her.

'Has it been that bad, Kate? I know Vicky can be a little monkey.'

Kate opened her mouth but no sound came out.

'Any coffee going?'

He gave a tired smile.

'What a night! Tim will pull through, though. He's tough.'

He reached the steps and stopped.

'Kate? What on earth . . . ?'

He dropped his jacket and grabbed her shoulders. 'What is it, Kate?'

'Vicky!' Kate's voice came out in a croak. 'I can't find her!'

His eyes blazed.

'What do you mean, you can't find her?'

'She's not here. She's disappeared!'

He went white.

'What?'

'I was about to ring the police. She was in the garden, and then she just disappeared.'

Tears gathered behind her eyes and she blinked them away.

'Are you sure? Have you looked everywhere?'

'Yes. She's not here. I feel so helpless.'

His sudden fury could not be contained.

'Helpless is hardly the word! How about incompetent? Not to mention criminally negligent? I trusted you, Kate! How could you do this?'

'But you surely don't think . . . look,

I'm extremely sorry this has happened.'

'Sorry? You'll be a lot sorrier if my daughter is not found! Have you done anything . . . informed the police?' He thrust her aside roughly and picked up the telephone and dialled a number.

'Description? Just a moment — '

He looked stonily at Kate, his eyebrows raised.

'Uh . . . red shirt, blue denims, brown pony tail.'

Within seconds, a cruising police car had stopped outside the gate and mechanically Kate answered the officer's questions, trying to keep her head. When the policeman got up to leave, Peter detained him.

'Wait. I'm coming with you.'

Grimly he turned to Kate.

'You can stay here in case she turns up.'

In the cold, furious eyes was a clear message. Distraught, Kate closed the door. She had never felt so wretched in her entire life. If anything had happened to Vicky she'd never forgive herself and if she couldn't forgive herself, however could she expect Peter Watson to? He had given her his trust and she had abused it. There would be a price to pay.

She sat down, her thoughts churning. Could some weirdo have enticed Vicky outside and abducted her? Had she been unforgivably negligent?

No, she decided in a moment of clarity, she hadn't! She'd even forbidden the child to leave the garden. But perhaps she should have checked on her more often, she agonised. Convinced of the worst, she closed her eyes and prayed for help. She then felt compelled to go out for one more look in the garden, in the vain hope she would see Vicky. But there was no sign of anyone.

Retracing her steps back into the house, her eyes were suddenly drawn to footprints in a wet patch which she'd watered that morning. They had been caused by a pair of high-heeled sandals!

Almost half an hour later, Peter

151

Watson stood on her doorstep, his face decidedly weary.

'I've come for Vicky's things,' he announced tightly.

'Yes, of course.'

Kate hurried down the passage and bundled the toothbrush, slippers and nightdress into the overnight bag.

'Here they are. I'm so terribly sorry — '

'Forget it,' he ground out.

'How can I?'

He brushed the words aside.

'I said forget it. The child has been found.'

'Thank goodness! Is — is she — '

'Unharmed? Yes, no thanks to you.'

'How can you say that?' Kate gulped. 'I've been through hell!'

'As have we all,' he spat out. 'You may save your guilt trip, your belated compunctions, Kate, as I have no intention of indulging them.'

He turned on his heel and walked away.

'Wait! I've said how sorry I am. You

must surely see that I . . . that things.'

She quailed at the blazing eyes but stood her ground.

'You must surely see that things were completely beyond my control.'

'They are indeed! You've been both inept and irresponsible. You're not fit to be entrusted with two beans in a jar, let alone somebody else's child. Goodbye, Miss Howard.'

Just like that! Kate couldn't believe her ears.

'One moment, Mr Watson. You have a right to be angry, but not downright unreasonable. Hear me out. You're being most unfair.'

'On the contrary. I have decided to take the matter no further, but let me tell you that if I were to inform the chairman of the school board of your negligence, you'd never be allowed near anyone's child again! If it were not for the speed with which Miss Barnard acted this morning, I shudder to think where Vicky would be at this moment. And you, Miss

Howard, would be facing charges!'

'Miss Barnard?' Kate shrilled. 'Just what has Miss Barnard to do with it?'

'Plenty. When I telephoned Hazelburn from the police station to inform my staff of the situation, Imelda answered. She told me to my utter relief that Vicky was quite safe. In fact, she was in the bath.'

'The bath?'

'Washing off the grime of the back streets of Bothatown. You will be interested to know that she was in a filthy condition when Imelda found her early this morning wandering about the less savoury parts. And did I mention that she was ravenously hungry, not having eaten since the previous evening?'

Kate swayed dizzily.

'But that's a downright lie!'

'And that she was incoherent with fright? No? Well, now you know. Oh, and one more thing! After this regrettable episode I intend to have Vicky assessed by a clinical psychologist.

Should she have come to any degree of psychological harm whatever, I shall be holding you personally responsible.'

He slammed the car door.

'I've never heard anything so preposterous!' Kate shrilled. 'You're badly mistaken. Hear me out, please. I think I know that Vicky was taken from my — '

The frantic appeal was drowned out by the roar of the exhaust.

Peter Watson's knuckles were white as he gripped the steering wheel savagely. He wasn't sure which was worse — rage or despair. So much for his hopes. How could he have been attracted to such a heartless, irresponsible woman?

On Monday morning, Kate still felt strained. She gave Pam instructions that should the chairman of the school board telephone, she was to be called immediately.

'Certainly,' Pam said, eager to know why. 'Trouble brewing?'

Kate gave an imitation of a carefree smile.

'Probably not.'

Trouble was an understatement! By lunch time, there could well be such a furore that her secretary's ears would be twitching, and by tomorrow, well, she refused to think about it.

By the end of the week, however, her job appeared to be still intact. Peter had kept his word. Not that she hadn't already decided that she would demand a fair hearing and be ready to go to any lengths to protect her professional reputation, of course. She had to. If Imelda's version of the story became common knowledge she'd never get another teaching post.

By mid-morning the office was becoming unbearably stuffy and Kate went out into the garden where she took a few deep breaths in order to consider her next move. She looked around for Vicky and spotted her amongst a group clustered around a jacaranda tree.

She appeared to be none the worse for wear after her ordeal.

'Vicky,' Kate said, drawing her unobtrusively aside, 'when you were playing in my garden with Sebastian the other day, did you manage to open that gate all by yourself?'

Vicky looked blank.

'Did Miss Barnard open the gate and come into the garden?'

Vicky nodded.

'And then what happened?'

'Then Sebastian jumped on to the wall by the lemon tree. He doesn't like Miss Barnard.'

'And then?'

'Then Miss Barnard said she would take me to buy an ice-cream. She wasn't cross any more, so I went.'

'I see. And then after you bought the ice-cream she took you straight home to Hazelburn in her yellow car, right?'

Vicky nodded.

'She said I could have a bubble bath with special bubbles as soon as we got home.'

She looked around, bored with the conversation.

'Shall I show you what I can do on the swing, Miss Howard?'

She skipped off, unable to comprehend in the least why Miss Howard considered what she'd said so important.

On Saturday morning, Kate drove into town. She had to find a suitable outfit for Sarah's dinner party that evening. She was successful in the first boutique she went to then headed for her father's store to purchase some suitable earrings.

Arriving at Sarah's, the new earrings glinted in the glow of the street lamp as she climbed out of her car. She was determined to enjoy the evening no matter who the surprise partner she knew Sarah had engineered for her turned out to be like. At least she was now back in circulation.

Kate locked the car, turned her head, and froze, for the dark grey BMW with the burgundy upholstery and distinctive number plate could only belong to one person, and she had not the slightest inclination ever to see him again, let alone spend an entire evening in the same room! But she couldn't run away now.

The rustle of her silk dress mingled with the sounds of the night as she negotiated the front path in her dainty evening shoes and paused for a moment to inhale the perfume of a flowering creeper nearby. Laughter spilled out with the pool of light from the open doorway.

'Kate! I thought I heard your car,' Sarah said as she answered the bell and drew her into the hall. 'My dear, you look marvellous! He'll be most impressed.'

He was indeed, and showed it. Under cover of the introductions, Luke Dalton's eyes devoured her as though she were a cream cake just waiting to be eaten. He was indeed a very good-looking young man.

'This is certainly a pleasure,' he said smoothly, taking Kate's hand. 'Where have you been all my life?'

She laughed. Mr Dalton might look like a movie star, but his corny lines rather spoiled the act. Accepting a glass of sherry, she sat down gracefully on the sofa and glanced around the room in time to see that a certain redhead had just choked on her drink while the tall, well-dressed man next to her was evidently experiencing rather a bad smell under the nose. Peter and Imelda could go and drown themselves, she thought sourly, none of which showed on her face.

By the time they all went in to dinner, Peter Watson had himself well under control. He could hardly take his eyes off Kate, fool that he was, and it helped not one bit to discover that she was to be seated beside him at dinner. He acknowledged her coldly and pulled out her chair.

Airily, Kate returned the greeting, shaking out her table napkin. She was determined that apart from the niceties there would be no further conversation.

'May I fill your glass?'

As Peter reached for the ice bucket, Imelda darted Kate a wary glance from across the table.

'Thank you.'

Without waiting any further, Kate plunged into conversation with the man seated on her left, a total stranger. Valiantly she attempted to do justice to Sarah's cooking but discovered annoyingly that her appetite had disappeared. Peter noticed it, too.

'Something wrong?' he mocked when she gave up on the raspberry mousse. 'You seem a little off your food this evening.'

Kate ignored him.

'Perhaps it's due to the fact that your glamour boy isn't seated by your side. I must say he's been trying hard enough with the blonde next to him.'

Kate held on to her temper.

'Keep your unremarkable observations to yourself, Mr Watson,' she gritted. 'They don't interest me in the least.'

His face darkened. He deserved that. What had got into him?

'Or better still,' Kate was suggesting, 'why not keep them for the green-eyed monster across the table? The devious lady who hangs on your every word.'

She heard his swiftly indrawn breath.

'I could be wrong, of course. Your Miss Barnard may be less devious than she looks.'

His blue eyes bored into her.

'Meaning?'

'Well, it was you, was it not, who enlightened me about appearances? They can be deceptive, you said, as many a noble soul lurks beneath an unlikely exterior. Take our friend, now. I'm sure she has an abundance of fine qualities, like charity and generosity and integrity. Not for one moment would she ever entertain any thought as unworthy as the intent to abduct, would she? She'd certainly never trespass on my property to kidnap a child, would she?'

Peter went very still.

'I would like an explanation of what you have just said,' he demanded quietly.

'It's a bit late in the day for explanations,' Kate said bitterly.

'Not as far as I'm concerned. What exactly are you implying?'

'Whatever I'm implying, Mr Watson, makes not the slightest bit of difference to anything. In my experience you will not see what you do not wish to see and you will not hear what you do not wish to hear.'

'Try me. An explanation is what I asked for, Miss Howard, and an explanation is what I'll get, if you please!'

'Take your hands off me at once,' Kate hissed, 'or I'll make a scene. You'll get no further explanation from now, nor in the future. I suggest you approach your daughter instead. She may just be the one person in this great, wide world who can put you straight.'

Next morning, Kate was awakened early by an insistent jangling of the telephone. She opened one eye and discovered it was scarcely eight o'clock.

'Yes?'

'Forgive the early hour. I would be grateful if I could come around this morning, Kate. I must speak to you.'

'We have nothing whatever to discuss, Mr Watson. Of all the effrontery, ringing me up like this!'

'Kate, I — '

She slammed down the phone and tried to go back to sleep. When the peace was shattered a second time she simply put the pillow over her head and let the telephone ring.

After lunch she headed off to see her parents.

10

Returning home, she parked outside the gate and fumbled in her bag for the front door key.

'Oh!'

She gave a squeal of fright. A large man was leaning against her door with his arms folded, obviously determined to wait all day if he had to. He winced.

'Am I that much of an ogre, Kate?'

Kate glared at Peter.

'What do you want?'

'May I come in?' he said, maintaining a sweet tone.

'Can you give me one good reason why I should?'

'Frankly, no. I've made a complete fool of myself and I've come to apologise. Now may I come in? I've spoken to Vicky. Please hear me out.'

'You wouldn't hear me out!'

Determinedly she shook his hand off

her arm and slammed the door.

Monday dawned bright and cloudless.

'Remember to rest when you go home,' Kate told the whole school, mindful of the heat build-up which was almost as bad as the mounting excitement. 'I want you all able to give of your best in the Nativity play this evening.'

A good turn-out of parents and friends was always expected at the play which was the highlight of the year. Kate could have done with a rest herself, but there was still too much to do. Cups and saucers had to be set out, the hall seating arranged and the percussion instruments placed in readiness for the small band which had been rehearsing all week.

At five-thirty, she was able to rush home for a quick shower and returned looking cool and confident in a well-cut blue velvet dress enhanced by a little simple jewellery. After inspecting the buffet which a dedicated band of mothers had arranged, Kate glanced at her watch and instructed the angels to stand in line for their wings to be fitted.

'Mrs Reddy will help you with the make-up,' she informed them, and from then on there was no more time for last-minute nervousness.

Vicky, the smallest angel, was next in line. She wore a troubled air.

'You look lovely,' Kate reassured her, thinking she was nervous. 'Remember how happy the angels on the hillside were? They were telling everybody the good news of Jesus' birth, so let's see that smile, Vicky.'

Vicky remained solemn.

'Miss Howard, why don't you like Uncle Peter?'

Kate gasped, at a loss for words.

'Who says I don't like him?' she stalled. 'He's a very interesting man.'

'But do you like him?'

Kate attached the angel wings with unsteady fingers.

'Why do you want to know?'

'Last night, I heard him tell Granny Elizabeth — '

She clapped a sudden hand over her mouth.

'Yes?'

But Vicky refused to elaborate.

'I wasn't s'posed to be listening.' She turned rather pink. 'I was s'posed to be in the bath.'

She ran to Mrs Reddy for her make-up.

The hall was soon filled. Kate seated herself at the piano and set about arranging her music. Taking a deep breath she began with some introductory music, her fingers sliding over the keyboard with the ease of many years' practice. After a few bars she lifted her head to glance around and faltered.

Peter Watson was sitting in the front row with his sister and an elegant, older woman who was regarding her with particular interest. Granny Elizabeth, Kate thought in some embarrassment. She wondered fleetingly what information it was that her son had seen fit to acquaint her with the previous evening. Really, children could be so maddening!

At that moment, however, they were nothing less than angelic, processing slowly down the aisle with lighted candles, singing their opening hymn. Then a hush fell as the Christmas story began to unfold.

Kate sipped a well-earned cup of coffee afterwards and was gratified to receive favourable comments from the proud parents.

'That was a curiously touching experience,' Peter Watson said softly. 'Don't rush off.' His fingers on her arm tightened. 'We need to talk.'

'There is nothing to talk about.'

'You won't listen, will you?'

'That's rich, coming from you.'

'I was badly mistaken and I've said so, with regret. What more do you want from me, Kate?'

'I want you to keep out of my life, Mr Watson.'

'Even during the season of goodwill?'

She couldn't quite meet his eyes. 'Yes.'

'In that case, I won't bother you again. Good-night.'

For the rest of the week, the children were kept busy making Christmas cards and decorations while the teachers completed their end-of-term duties. When Kate made her final tour of inspection she was able to congratulate them on a job well done.

When the alarm clock went off on Friday morning, Kate could not quite believe that her last day at the school had come. It was to be a short morning after which she would be reminding the children that their old principal, Mrs Rattray, would be there to welcome them back after the holidays.

She dressed with a sense of anti-climax and drove to Happy Days where she was presented with a variety of gifts and cards which touched her with their little messages of love and appreciation. She was just receiving Jason's bunch of flowers when Vicky marched in with a beautifully-wrapped pink box.

'Open it, Miss Howard.'

She was hopping up and down with excitement.

'It's from me and Uncle Peter.'

Kate's hand trembled as she lifted the lid.

'It's beautiful,' she gasped.

The small, exquisitely carved ivory elephant lying in her palm gleamed.

'Do you like it?' Vicky needed further assurance.

'I love it.'

She gave the child a quick hug and slipped the accompanying card back into the box. When she read it again later the words stared back at her, a very strange message indeed.

O, Kate, content thee: prithee, be not angry . . .

The teachers were torn between relief and sadness as their charges were collected for the last time. Kate's own feeling of accomplishment was tinged with an unaccountable depression and every time she caught sight of Vicky

Watson the anguish grew. It wouldn't be long before Alpheus arrived and bore the little girl away for ever. But it was not Alpheus who came striding through the door a few minutes later.

'My driver was not available,' Peter explained.

Kate wondered why he was going to such lengths to see her again. Kate decided she would be polite if it killed her.

'Thank you for Vicky's gift, Mr Watson. It was very thoughtful. I like elephants.'

'I know.'

He noted every detail of her face as though imprinting it upon his memory.

'It will serve to remind me of Vicky.'

'That was the idea.'

Kate hid her feelings as she hugged the child and tried to swallow the lump in her throat.

'Take care, Vicky,' she whispered.

'Oh, but I don't have to say goodbye to you now, Miss Howard. I'll see you at Hazelburn because you're getting an invitation to my birthday party.'

She skipped happily down the front steps. Helplessly Kate turned to Peter Watson.

'Please understand that I will not be there, Mr Watson.'

He smiled mirthlessly.

'I didn't think you would, Kate. But before I go I just want to tell you that I have spoken at length with Imelda. She has since returned to Cape Town, permanently.'

Kate was coldly polite.

'Thank you for informing me, but it's actually none of my business.'

'I believe it is.'

'You are very much mistaken. I have no further interest in you or your mistress.'

'Mistress?'

There was a flash of genuine astonishment before his eyes grew cold.

'You are the one who is mistaken, Kate. I've been trying to escape Imelda's unwelcome advances for months. The woman's been a confounded nuisance.'

'Goodbye, Mr Watson,' Kate said sweetly. 'Vicky is waiting for you.'

The promised invitation to Vicky's party duly arrived. Kate immediately set about replying. Vicky would be disappointed, of course, but she'd soon forget. She mooched around the house for two days trying to find things to do. Her social life amounted to nothing at present.

By Wednesday, Kate decided to ring her father and beg to be allowed to work in the business. Mr Howard was grateful for the offer.

Each day she arrived at work earlier than the rest of the staff and insisted on staying until late even though her feet were aching by the end of the day. She was losing weight, too, anyone could see that.

It was two days before Christmas when an elegant woman came into the shop and looked about her as thought expecting to see someone in particular. Kate hurried forward, wondering where she had seen her before.

'I'm looking for a watch for my granddaughter.'

Shrewd blue eyes appraised her closely before she smiled, apparently satisfied.

'What age is she?' Kate enquired.

It was no use showing her a watch for a teenager if the child was much younger.

'Oh, er, four.'

Despite the old lady's vagueness Kate had the feeling there was very little she missed.

'No, five. Silly of me! It was her birthday last week, of course. I do believe you know her, my dear. Victoria Watson.'

Kate started.

'Of course. Then you must be — '

'Elizabeth Watson. How do you do? Now, what can you show me?'

Kate bent over the counter to hide her consternation as she drew out a tray.

'What about this one, Mrs Watson? The numbers are clear and the strap is fairly colourful. It's quite sturdy, too, for a first watch.'

'Excellent. They will all be spending Christmas Day with me and I shall let her have it then. She particularly wanted a watch for Christmas, and I'm sure she won't be disappointed with your choice. Thank you, my dear.'

'Would you like it gift-wrapped?' Kate offered politely. 'We have some pretty pink paper.'

'That would be most kind.'

'Have a lovely Christmas, Mrs Watson, and give my love to Vicky.'

She wasted no time in handing over the parcel and hurrying off to her next customer.

'What's this?' Margo shrilled a few moments later.

Kate straightened up from replacing a tray of rings in the cabinet.

'What?' she asked.

'This parcel. I found it here near the till. Surely you must have seen who left it behind.'

'I don't keep tabs on each and every

person who comes into the shop, Margo,' she retorted, 'but in this case I do happen to know who it belongs to. A Mrs Watson. No doubt she'll realise what's happened and come back for it. I suggest you just leave it under the counter.'

But the package still lay unclaimed the following day. Knowing there was no firm's delivery to Pietermaritzburg Kate realised Vicky would not receive her watch over Christmas. She spoke without thinking.

'I know where the child lives. I could drop it off, I suppose.'

It would at least be there for her when she got back from her grandmother's and with the Watsons out of the way in Pietermaritzburg, she'd be quite safe to call. It would make a pleasant drive after church in the morning and give her something to do before going to her parents' home for Christmas dinner.

Stepping outside after work was like a blast from a furnace. Hot wind stung her eyes and whipped her hair into knots. She flung herself into the car and leaned across to switch on the radio.

'Conditions are worsening in most of the interior,' a voice was intoning, 'with parts which are still desperately dry. A Red Alert has been established as fire conditions are prevalent.'

Christmas morning dawned hot and restless. Kate awoke feeling unrefreshed and took another shower. The wind was unabated and they were in for another long, uncomfortable day.

The church was packed for the early service as the vicar had warned that it was to be broadcast, but Kate managed to find a seat near the back and joined in the opening carol with as much energy as the sapping humidity would allow.

By the time her car later nosed out of the quiet town towards Hazelburn, Kate was already dying of thirst. She planned to deliver the package to Albertina and leave immediately. The sooner she could relax at her parents' home with a glass of iced punch, the better.

Smoothly changing into top gear she leaned back to enjoy the drive. There were a few things she needed to think about, not least the vicar's sermon on forgiveness. The wind, she noticed in dismay, was peaking at around seventy kilometers per hour and the car kept veering to the right. Easing the car as close to the house as she could when she arrived at her destination, she opened the door only to have it fly almost off its hinges. Then, clutching the small pink package together with her flying skirts, she ran up the veranda steps and lifted a rather frenzied hand to the bell.

She gasped as strong arms engulfed her suddenly and unceremoniously, pulling her into the shelter of the house and holding her against a broad chest while the door crashed shut, driven by a furious gust.

'Merry Christmas, Kate,' Peter Watson mocked.

'Merry Christmas. But what are you doing here?'

He feigned amazement.

'I live here, remember?'

'Yes, but . . . '

'But what?'

'You're supposed to be spending the day in Pietermaritzburg,' she accused. 'Your mother said so.'

It was his turn to gape.

'My mother? Since when, Kate Howard, have you taken to holding conversation with my mother?'

'I . . . well, all I know is that Mrs Watson came into the shop and bought Vicky a watch for Christmas. She said Vicky particularly wanted it, and then she went and left the parcel on the counter.'

'Did she, the wily old bird!'

'Yes.'

It would appear that the mother was just as determined as the son for them to be thrown together!

'She said you would be having Christmas with her!'

His shoulders were shaking.

'So you thought it would be safe enough to come out to Hazelburn and deliver the parcel. Well, well.'

Angrily Kate thrust the package into his hands.

'Here. Goodbye, Mr Watson.'

He grabbed her arm and propelled her firmly into the living-room.

'Don't you know that a farmer always makes hay while the sun shines? Now that you're here, Kate Howard, I intend to make the most of it. Let me at least offer you a glass of iced tea, or would you prefer something more festive?'

'No, thank you.'

Her voice was as icy as the cubes he was already clinking into a glass.

'I really don't think that I care to be manipulated any further by the Watson family.'

He gave a sudden grin.

'That's reasonable. Relax, Kate, all will be explained. I was invited to Pietermaritzburg along with the rest of the family, but declined and sent Vicky along with Gillian. There's a Red Alert on.'

'Yes, I heard.'

'When there's a fire warning, you don't risk leaving.'

Thirstily, she drained her glass and put it down. It was rude of her, but she needed to get away.

'Thank you for the drink, Mr Watson. I'm afraid I must go.'

'Not before we've spoken,' he said calmly. 'There are things we need to straighten out.'

'No! I can talk as much as I like but you simply don't listen, and now it's too late.'

Kate swallowed back the tears as she drove resolutely back to Bothatown so that by the time she reached her parents' home her smile was firmly in place. Together they opened their lovingly chosen gifts and chatted about everything.

After dinner, they sat at the poolside until Toby began to agitate for his walk.

'Come on then, you old rascal,' Mr

Howard told him, draining his cup and escorting the elderly animal to the garden gate.

Mrs Howard turned immediately to her daughter.

'What is it, love? There's something bothering you. I don't wish to pry, but airing things sometimes helps.'

She and her friend Elizabeth might have a shrewd idea how the land lay between their respective offspring but she forbore to say as much. Kate would have to make the first move.

'I do have a problem,' she admitted, curiously relieved to be able to speak about it, 'and more so since hearing the vicar's sermon this morning. He said something about Christmas being a time to love. A time to forgive.'

'I remember.'

'Well,' she burst out, 'it's all a bit much! I can't do it.'

'Can't, or won't?'

Kate was startled.

'What do you mean?'

'Well, there will always be plenty of

people who hurt you in life, just as you are bound to hurt others. Letting go of the anger which someone has caused you and making a conscious decision to forgive is a very costly thing to do but it's the only way to wholeness and therefore to happiness. Think about it.'

'But what if the person doesn't deserve to be forgiven?'

'None of us deserves to be forgiven, and nobody's perfect.'

'So what you're saying is, don't wait for other people to be perfect before you forgive them because it will never happen.'

Her mother nodded.

'You have to make the first move. Do what you know to be right, Kate, and it will pay off in the long run.'

Thoughtfully Kate stared into the pool. It looks as though she would shortly be taking another trip out to Hazelburn, and it wouldn't be easy.

The late afternoon sun was every bit as fierce as the morning's had been. For the second time that day Kate bumped her way along Peter Watson's road. She had as yet no clear idea of what she wanted to say and almost decided to turn back. The wind, somewhat abated, was still gusting through the pastures and as her eyes adjusted to the sun's glare they suddenly widened. It wasn't the sun which was blinding her, but a great orange flame stabbing the distant sky where there should have been a line of hills.

'No!'

In terror, she accelerated through the dust towards the farmhouse and flung herself from the car.

'Mr Watson . . . Peter!' she screamed, stumbling up the veranda steps.

He had already heard the car and was moving towards the front door in astonishment.

'What the . . . ?'

'Over there,' she croaked, dragging him to the living-room window.

She heard his quick intake of breath, followed by an awful stillness as he stared disbelievingly at flames spewing into the air and leaping across the hills towards the open veld beyond the house, fanned by the wind. Galvanised into action, he reached for a box of matches on the mantelpiece.

'Stay here, Kate. I'll have to backburn from the house. It's our only chance.'

'No! I'm coming, too.'

She sped after him, too frightened to think. They ran to the shed for a can of petrol and tore down the slope to the end of the garden where the veld began. Together they doused a line of grass along its edge and ignited it so that within minutes it, too, became an inferno, racing through the tinder-dry grass towards the oncoming fire.

'Soak the lawn,' Peter yelled, indicating a garden hose, 'and then do the thatch. The herd is in the milking enclosure. They're safe enough.'

He disappeared around the side of the house. Kate did as she was told, panting with exertion. Amy and Sheena were barking from the living-room window, excited but safe.

As soon as she could, she followed him around the corner and ran straight into Zondi, a retired herdsman who was on duty over the festive season. He had just emerged from the shed, his eyes round with fear.

'Wait! Don't let the cows out!' Kate yelled, and he immediately ran to secure the gate.

Then in agitation he pointed. Kate trained her eyes on the figure racing towards the bottom pasture and her heart stood still. The fire was roaring towards a group of calves whose destruction he was obviously intent on preventing.

Peter was igniting the patch to be backburned and hadn't noticed the gate which had blown open. One or two of the animals were already making for it, terrified by both the noise and the smell. Kate kicked off her high heeled sandals and ran like a springbok, leaping blindly over stones and anthills, uncaring. If the smoke was burning the calves' eyes as it was hers, no wonder they were frantic.

At all costs, she must stop them reaching that gate. It was pointless saving them on one boundary only to let them succumb on the other.

Peter watched, satisfied, as the new flames roared backwards towards the body of the fire leaving bare, smouldering earth in their wake. At least that would halt the fire's progress. He turned to ignite the other boundary and saw Kate streaking along the fence.

'Back,' Peter yelled, thrusting a handkerchief over her mouth.

He urged her along a path, the only access left which avoided the hot, blackened earth. By this time her feet were cut and bruised and when she stumbled he simply picked her up and quickened his stride.

'They've seen us, thank God!'

'Who?'

'Fire Protection Services.'

He was breathing heavily as he lowered her on to the soggy but untouched lawn in front of the house. Aircraft appeared from nowhere and began to release their loads of water and chemicals, causing even more smoke to billow over the countryside.

★   ★   ★

'Drink this,' Peter said some time later.

Kate looked at him and gave a near-hysterical giggle, for his blackened face was grotesquely streaked where the perspiration had run in rivulets down his skin. She took a large gulp and tried to keep her hands from shaking.

When at last she joined him at the living-room window, the wind had dropped, leaving an eerie silence. Everywhere was utter devastation. Only the bottom pasture remained intact, its huddle of calves now grazing calmly. The dairy herd, too, had escaped, shut into the milking enclosure.

'What will you do now, Peter?' she asked worriedly.

'Everything is insured, but it's not

the money. It will take years to get reestablished and at this moment I'm not at all sure I have the motivation.'

He looked utterly weary.

'I'll help you,' Kate offered impulsively. 'You can't give up now.'

He smiled.

'You're a sweet girl but you're in a state of shock.'

'You have your home intact.'

'Sure. I'm very grateful, and I escaped with my life, although,' he made an attempt at levity, 'my clothes will never be quite the same again.'

He surveyed her closely.

'If you're feeling OK now, I suggest you use the ensuite bathroom to clean up and then we'll put something on those feet. After that I'll drive you home. You can leave your car here. I'll have it delivered tomorrow when Alpheus is back.'

He disappeared down the passage to take a shower and Kate followed.

'Ready?'

Peter stood politely as she re-entered

the living-room some time later. He wore clean jeans and a crisp shirt, his hair still damp and his face sombre. Kate sat down calmly on the sofa.

'No,' she told him calmly, 'I'm not.'

She couldn't go without saying what she'd come to say. It was now or never.

'I suppose it had occurred to you that I didn't drive all the way out to Hazelburn to tell you there was a fire.'

'When you didn't even know there would be one? Yes, it had occurred to me. Whatever it is you came to say can be said in the car. Shall we go?'

'Listen to me, Peter Watson, for once in your life! You are the most maddening, pig-headed male I've ever met, do you know that? You're always jumping to conclusions about me and I've had enough.'

'Like I said,' he drawled, pushing her through the door, 'you may appraise me of all that on the way back.'

Fuming, Kate preceded him to the car. She fastened her seat-belt wanting to say so much and not knowing quite where to start. In his present mood he was hardly likely to listen to a word, either. He had turned off the main track on to an unfamiliar one which seemed to lead to the hill above the house.

'Where are you going?'

'To the top.'

'Why?'

'What an infuriating girl you are! We are going there because much as I hate to look, it will give me a view over the whole farm.'

'Oh.'

As they bumped to a halt, Kate realised she had been holding her breath and let it out on a long sigh. They sat in silence and surveyed the smoking landscape while thunder sounded ominously in the distance.

'What now?' Kate demanded.

'We'll have some rain on top of all this soggy mess and the countryside will take weeks to recover. In a day or two the insurance people will descend to assess this lot and will doubtless haggle for weeks. For the present there is nothing I can do until my workforce returns.'

'I really am sorry,' Kate whispered.

'Thank you, but don't lose any sleep over it. As you so rightly pointed out, I still have my home, and I'm committed to it, like I am to my family.'

'You take family ties seriously, don't you?'

'Too much so, at times,' he admitted, 'and I've been a fool about some things, like Vicky. We live and learn, don't we?'

'Yes.'

'What have you learned recently then, Kate?' he mocked.

'I've learned,' she told him slowly, 'about forgiving people.'

Something flickered in his eyes.

'Elaborate.'

'Well, the lack of forgiveness keeps you chained to the past in the wrong way so that you can't get on with your life. I want to get on with mine.'

His face revealed nothing of the sudden hope which leaped within him.

'Go on.'

'When you're hating someone or something in your past and refusing to let go of it, it kind of cripples you for the future. Do you understand what I'm saying?'

'I do indeed. I've been carrying a fair amount of it myself. Sours the mind.'

Kate gave him a brilliant smile, so that he blinked. It was a new feeling, this mutual understanding, and to her own amazement she wanted it to continue.

'I'd like to tell you about it, Kate. It began with Felicia. You see, I loved her.'

He gazed at the blackened plantations once green with pines.

'But like that forest, it turned to ashes, especially after she'd met my brother. She wanted his money, you see. As the eldest he stood to inherit this place. That's why I had to offer his child a home, don't you see?'

'Yes.'

'I was a humble English lecturer, Kate, and Felicia a drama student. She

194

could be a very captivating lady and frankly, I was smitten. Afterwards I hated the two of them.'

'Until you realised what she was really like.'

He turned to look at her.

'Exactly. Then Mark became ill. There's nothing like terminal illness to clear the air, is there? I asked him to forgive me but he said he was the one who needed forgiveness for taking her away. I told him it no longer mattered but even after he died I still felt guilty. After the funeral I automatically assumed that Vicky would be happier with her mother, so I did nothing about the promise I'd made to care for her. I couldn't have been more wrong. When I found out about Vicky I was wretched. I felt I still owed Mark, and I was fraught about the child's well-being. It was an intolerable load and it was destroying me.'

It had grown dark and Peter moved to switch on the ignition.

'I'd better take you home.'

'Wait,' Kate said. 'I want to tell you about the baggage I dumped. After that day you accused me of negligence, I was extremely angry with you, Peter. You believed Imelda. You doubted my integrity, my professionalism. You doubted my word!'

'Like I said, I've been a fool. I'm sorry.'

He switched on the engine.

'Let's go.'

Kate reached across him and turned it off.

'Don't you even want to know what I really came to speak to you about? I came to ask you if we could make a fresh beginning, Peter. Because I love you.'

He appeared stunned.

'Would you say that again, Miss Howard?'

'I love you, Peter Watson.'

'I have a strict policy,' he managed to say, 'never to argue with a school teacher. But there is something which I find absolutely non-negotiable.'

'And that is?'

' "Thou must be married to no man but me",' he quoted once again from Shakespeare. ' "I must and will have Katharine to my wife".'

'But I'm none too keen on a husband who sits up all night reading Shakespeare, let alone quote it at me all the time, instead of . . . '

He continued to regard her steadily.

'Instead of?'

Kate blushed.

'Well, kissing me, for a start, Peter.'

'If I promise to kiss you, for a start, will you help me with the calves, the coots, two German shepherds and one small girl, not to mention various other little Watsons in due course?'

'I will.' Kate laughed.

' "Why, there's a wench",' Peter whispered, once again quoting Shakespeare. 'Come on, and kiss me, Kate.'

We do hope that you have enjoyed reading this large print book.

Did you know that all of our titles are available for purchase?

We publish a wide range of high quality large print books including:
Romances, Mysteries, Classics
General Fiction
Non Fiction and Westerns

Special interest titles available in large print are:
The Little Oxford Dictionary
Music Book, Song Book
Hymn Book, Service Book

Also available from us courtesy of Oxford University Press:
Young Readers' Dictionary
(large print edition)
Young Readers' Thesaurus
(large print edition)

For further information or a free brochure, please contact us at:
Ulverscroft Large Print Books Ltd.,
The Green, Bradgate Road, Anstey,
Leicester, LE7 7FU, England.
Tel: (00 44) **0116 236 4325**
Fax: (00 44) **0116 234 0205**

FINGALA, MAID OF RATHAY

Mary Cummins

On his deathbed, Sir James Montgomery of Rathay asks his daughter, Fingala, to swear that she will not honour her marriage contract until her brother Patrick, the new heir, returns from serving the King. Patrick must marry. Rathay must not be left without a mistress. But Patrick has fallen in love with the Lady Catherine Gordon whom the King, James IV, has given in marriage to the young man who claims to be Richard of York, one of the princes in the Tower.

ZABILLET OF THE SNOW

Catherine Darby

For Zabillet, a young peasant girl growing up in the tiny French village of Fromage in the mid-fourteenth century, a respectable marriage is the height of her parents' ambitions for her. But life is changing. Zabillet's love for a handsome shepherd is tested when she is invited to join the La Neige household, where her mistress, Lady Petronella, has plans for her grandson, Benet. And over all broods the horror of the Great Death that claims all whom it touches.

BOSTON PUBLIC LIBRARY

3 9999 04662 652 7

7/03

G1

PERILOUS JOURNEY

Caroline Joyce

After the execution of Charles I, Louisa's Royalist father considers it too dangerous for her to stay in England and arranges for her to go to the Isle of Man with Armand de la Tremouille, the nephew of the island's Royalist Governor. Their ship is boarded by Parliamentarians who plan to sail for Ireland, but a storm causes them to be shipwrecked on the Calf of Man. Magnus Stapleton, the Parliamentarian chief, becomes infatuated with Louisa, but she has fallen in love with Armand.

WITHDRAWN
No longer the property of the
Boston Public Library.
Sale of this material benefits the Library.